A Place of Grace

By Darlia Sawyer

Copyright © 2018
Written by: Darlia Sawyer
Published by: Forget Me Not Romances, a division of Winged Publications

This book is a work of fiction. Names, characters, places, and incidents are the product of the author's imagination and are used fictitiously. Any resemblance to actual events, locales, or persons, living or dead, is coincidental.

All rights reserved.

ISBN-13: **979-8-3493-0404-0**

Acknowledgements

We often wonder why dreams don't happen when we want them to. The reasons for this could be many but we wait on God's timing. It could be because we haven't gained the wisdom needed or the right people to make it possible haven't come into our lives. God blessed me with a husband who goes beyond what most would do to see my dreams become a reality. I appreciate all the countless hours he puts into editing with me to make the book better. You are loved.

Chapter One

1901

Drake West balanced himself on a rickety wooden fence, pushed his flat-brimmed Stetson back on his head and scanned the beautiful Montana valley. He'd lived here with his wife, Noel, for the last two years.

Crystal clear icicles hung from tall pine trees beneath the snow-covered mountains reminding him the fierceness of winter would soon arrive. As he gazed on the surrounding beauty, his heart ached because of the mess his marriage had become.

Should he spend another night at the sheriff's office or choose the sofa in his sitting room at home? He kept a cot at the jail because as sheriff he'd spent many nights there watching the prisoners. Only recently had he been able to hire a deputy to give him time off.

Six years ago today, he married the woman of his dreams, Noel Anderson. She'd been born on December twenty-fifth and was her parents most treasured Christmas present for almost twenty-seven years.

Drake met Noel at the First Baptist Church in Denver, Colorado, and they courted shortly after. Her long curly hair was the color of sunflowers at dawn. When he held her hand for the first time he knew she was the one.

They didn't have children, so they filled their lives with their two collies, Tucker and Maggie. The collies demanded attention with their endless licks and obsession with playing fetch. Drake and Noel also adopted a kitten named, Coco, to keep the mice down. She was a stray they found while riding through the beautiful wildflowers that covered this area of the valley in the spring. She hadn't been the best mouser, but she kept the dogs moving by pouncing on them when they'd get comfortable. Their quarter horses, Gunner and Ruby had been good to them. Drake had considered breeding them so they could raise their foals and sell them.

His time with Noel had been the happiest years of his life until they moved to Bozeman, Montana. As the only law officer in the town, it kept him busier than he'd expected. When he worked in Denver as a Deputy Sheriff it had required long hours but nothing like here. For the last year, Drake had asked the mayor to employ another deputy, but the mayor denied his request each time. Drake finally put his foot down and threatened to quit but hiring, Albert Burns, may have come too late to save his marriage.

Footsteps crackled near him and a tree branch snapped, Drake reached for his gun.

"Put down gun, Drake. It's, Kitchi." The dark-skinned young man yelled as he stepped out from the bushes behind him. Drake holstered his gun and embraced the Crow warrior. Kitchi had become the brother he'd always wished for.

His mother said Drake was blessed to have three older sisters, but blessed was not the right word. He would've used the word cursed, too many dolls and afternoon tea parties.

Drake grew up wanting to be like his father. He'd been a sergeant in the Civil War for the Union Army. His father didn't talk about those days much, the soldiers lived through a very difficult time. He recognized the courage it took to face the possibility of death each day.

When Drake and Noel first moved to Montana, a cattle rustler shot him. If Kitchi hadn't found him and took him to his camp, he would have bled to death. Unconscious for two days, Kitchi tended to his wounds. When he opened his eyes, he didn't remember being shot but realized he owed Kitchi a debt he could never repay.

Kitchi spoke pretty good English. A missionary couple lived near their camp and taught them about God and how to speak in English. The Crow had realized the benefits of being friendly with the white man early on. They welcomed Drake while he recovered, for the most part.

"Why you up here?" Kitchi slapped Drake on the back. "Nothing to do?"

"Plenty to do. I needed time to think. This spot in the high county always brings me peace." Drake dug his heel into the layer of snow on the ground exposing the dirt underneath.

Kitchi leaned against the fence next to him. "More problems with wife?"

"Yep, more of the same with Noel. I think she'd be happier without me. I love her, but don't know how to make it better." Drake couldn't explain to Kitchi what he didn't understand.

"Have you talked to Great Spirit about it?" Kitchi straightened out the strings of blue beads that fell in rows down the front of his antelope skin tunic.

"I doubt if He's interested in my problems, so many other people to care for." Drake stepped toward his horse. "You riding into town today?"

"No, hunting. Big storm moving in so need more meat. Bad winter coming." Kitchi whistled and his black and white Paint horse, Flying Wind, came running to him.

"What signs tell you winter will be bad?" Drake fed his horse Gunner an apple. "I need to cut more wood if that's true."

"Can tell by animals. They store lots of food. Would be wise to do the same." Kitchi rubbed his Paint's nose. The horse snorted.

Drake tossed an apple to Kitchi. "He's jealous."

"You spoil Gunner. Make him soft." Kitchi held out the apple and Flying Wind ate it.

"Keeps him loyal. You never know when you need them to stay with you." Drake laughed. "Well Kitchi, I should head back. Hopefully, the town is still standing."

"Ride strong. Be brave." Kitchi jumped on his horse and galloped into the forest.

Drake envied his friends freedom to hunt, trap

and ride all day. No one to complain about their neighbor taking their chicken eggs or stealing their underwear off the clothesline. But, those were the easy days. The ones he dreaded most were when someone came up missing or were murdered. He'd dealt with things no man should have to see.

Noel didn't understand how he let his job consume him until he could barely breathe. It left him struggling for a way to bring justice to situations that would never be justified. Drake had learned evil ran rampant in men and women's hearts.

He nudged Gunner and headed toward Bozeman in the valley below. The sun's rays tried to heat the cold air but they'd soon be retiring for the night. Drake saw smoke rising in the distance, duty called. He wouldn't be heading back to town after all.

Chapter Two

Noel picked up her plate from the dining room table. Another dinner alone. Drake told her he'd be home tonight as Deputy Albert would be on duty. She'd hoped after hiring Albert they might be able to spend more time together. So far she hadn't noticed a difference in how little time he spent with her. He always had a good reason to be away, or so he reasoned.

Tucker and Maggie begged at her feet as she put the remainder of her barely touched dinner into their bowls. She loved the Collies, they'd been her faithful companions during her nights alone. She couldn't forget to give Coco a few bites too. The orange tabby spent her evenings curled up on the sofa waiting for Noel to join her in front of the warm fire.

Noel's parents had separated, and each had their own house now. It was the latest scandal to hit Denver society columns because her father had been seen with another woman. Noel hadn't visited her parents since Drake and she had moved to Bozeman two years ago. She missed spending time with them. Noel wanted to ask Drake if she could go to Denver in the spring to see them. Denver had always been her home. *Why would he care? It'd take him a week to realize I was gone.* If Noel went back, she'd have to hire someone to run her bakeshop. She didn't know who could do that.

The bakeshop had become her baby, so to speak, since she and Drake had not yet had children. Not being a mother didn't bother her, especially when mothers came in with their young children and they were getting into everything. A mother never stopped working. If Noel had little ones, they'd be well-behaved. She'd been spoiled as an only child but her parents never let her act out.

Occasionally, Noel wished her parents hadn't let Drake court her. They warned her he'd whisk her away to some faraway place, and she'd rarely see her family or have the type of life she'd been accustomed to. Of course, all she could see was a handsome deputy with big muscles and golden-brown eyes.

She had dreamed of all they'd do together. Since moving to Bozeman, he'd only made it home a couple nights out of the week. She couldn't remember his last full day off. Noel started the bakeshop to be around people, instead of being alone.

As a young girl, she had enjoyed baking even though her parents employed a cook. Miss Maples was loved by her family, and she liked having Noel help her in the kitchen. She talked all the time and taught Noel how to cook. Now Noel shared everything, Miss Maples taught her with the residents of Bozeman. Her bakeshop was busy, and she might need to hire a helper soon.

A soft tapping on the front door woke Noel from her musings. She opened it to find, Violet, her next-door neighbor, standing there with a pair of oven mitts.

"I've been working on these oven mitts for you for a couple of weeks. I made a pair for myself too. I didn't see Drake's horse, so figured you were alone. I should've checked earlier and invited you over for dinner."

"Thank you so much, Violet. They are beautiful, I will use them at the bakeshop. You cheer me up on my worst days. Yes, I'm alone, as usual." Noel met Violet shortly after she and Drake moved to Bozeman and they became best friends. Violet had never married, and she wasn't sure she wanted to. She helped a local dressmaker when the mood struck her. Her parents passed away last year and left her a wealthy inheritance, enough that Violet never had to worry about working. They were the same age and Noel was grateful for her friendship.

Violet followed Noel to the kitchen. "It must be important for Drake to be away. He'd rather be home with you."

"I'm not sure any more, Violet. I believed that at first but sometimes it feels like Drake doesn't care. I even wonder if he is interested in another woman." Noel filled a tea kettle with water. "Have a seat at the table. We can have tea and leftover scones from the bakeshop. They're apple, your favorite."

"Drake would never cheat on you. He loves you way too much. I see it in his eyes every time he looks at you. You don't like being alone, but never doubt his love for you. Now that he hired Albert, I'm sure things will get better."

"I wish I had your confidence. I dwell too much on what might be going on. How was your afternoon walk?" Noel set a plate of scones on the table.

"It was exhilarating. The weather is cold, but I bundled up and enjoyed the crisp fall air. There's not a lot of leaves left on the trees and the snow is deep in some places. I'm not ready to be snowed in. Hopefully, we'll have a mild winter. Were you busy at the bakeshop?"

"Very. I may need to hire someone to help me with the holidays coming up. Especially in the mornings as I make everything for the day then. If you aren't helping at the dress shop, you should come help me."

Noel poured hot water into their cups and took a seat across from Violet. The tea and sugar were on the table. "Have a scone, I made them fresh this morning. I hardly touched my dinner earlier, but since you came over I'm feeling hungry."

Violet took a bite of her apple scone. "Mmmm, these are delicious! You are a good baker. I understand why so many people are coming to your shop. I haven't been at the dress shop lately, but with the weather turning cold I'll be working more.

We sew a lot during the winter when there isn't much else to do but be inside. I'd never make it into the bakeshop as early as you get there. I'm barely falling asleep then." Violet sipped her tea. "It's hot."

"I would hope so." Noel blew in her cup to cool it. "We should put snow it in."

"With all the animals around here, I don't want to risk getting the yellow kind." Violet laughed and took another bite.

A knock on the door interrupted their conversation and Noel answered it.

"Good evening, Mrs. West."

"Good evening, Pastor Sheffield. How are you?"

"I'm a little concerned. Would Drake happen to be here? I stopped by the sheriff's office first, but Deputy Albert said he hasn't seen him. We were supposed to meet tonight, and it's not like him to miss." Tucker snuck up behind the Pastor, trying to be the guard dog he was trained to be.

"He hasn't come home yet and I haven't heard from him either. I assumed he was at the jail." Noel tried to get Tucker to go back over by her but the stubborn dog refused.

"I sure hope everything's all right. If he's not back by morning, let me know and we'll look for him. My wife and I will be praying." Pastor Sheffield backed up a couple of steps.

"Thanks for coming by and checking on him, it was very thoughtful. I'll tell you if he doesn't come home. He's often away overnight, for one crisis or another, so it's probably something like that." Noel whistled softly but Tucker just sat behind the Pastor.

"I'm sorry, it must be hard on you having him gone so much. You're always welcome at our house for dinner if you can put up with the noise from six young children. They're all very well-behaved but they have their moments. I'll let you get back to what you were doing. Remember if you need anything please don't hesitate to come by. Good night, Noel." Pastor Sheffield almost tripped over Tucker when he turned around.

"Thanks for your generous offer, pastor. I may take you up on it one of these nights." Noel looked down and noticed a small box sitting by the door.

"We'd love to have you." Pastor Sheffield walked down the path to the gate.

"Have a good night." Noel picked up the box, it was addressed to her. She went inside and closed the door.

"Who was at the door? What's in the box?" Violet asked when Noel walked into the kitchen.

"Pastor Sheffield asked if Drake was here. He missed a meeting with him. This package was outside, and it's addressed to me. I wonder what it is."

"Are you worried something is wrong with Drake? That package wasn't there when I came over." Violet drank the last of her tea. "Open it."

"He probably got held up somewhere, as happens all the time. Although, it's not like him to miss a meeting. I wish he'd tell me what he's doing so I don't have to guess. If Drake isn't back by morning, Pastor Sheffield, will get some men to look for him. Noel opened the box and picked up a tissue wrapped object.

"I wonder if Drake left it as a surprise since he wouldn't be home." Violet scooted her chair closer to Noel.

Noel carefully unwrapped the item. An exquisite red glass heart glistened at her. There wasn't a card or note attached. "If it was Drake, it would be a change of character. Unless it's my birthday, our anniversary, or Christmas, he rarely gives me a gift just to surprise me."

"It's beautiful. Who else would give you something like this?" Violet picked up the heart.

Noel's mind went back to yesterday when the owner of the bank, Mr. Steele, had come into the bakeshop. He'd been pleasant to her, almost flirtatious. When she handed him the change from his order, he held her hand for a few seconds. It caught her off guard and she didn't know how to react. When she looked up at him, he smiled and said goodbye.

Surely, he wouldn't leave a gift at her doorstep, knowing she was married. No, it must be Drake. He wanted to make up for being gone tonight. Although, why didn't he tell her what was keeping him away? None of this made any sense.

"You're right, it has to be Drake. It's kind of mysterious as to why he didn't come in and give it to me." Noel sat and sipped her tea. "My tea is cold, is yours? I'll heat up some more water. This is awful."

Chapter Three

Drake fell to the ground, driving his face into the cold mountain stream, gulping water down his parched throat until it made him choke. The intensity of the last few hours caught up to him.

The fire was at the McGregor's farm. Both the home and barn were completely engulfed in flames when he arrived. He kept it from spreading to adjacent farmland but came upon the semi-charred and bullet-ridden bodies of Mr. McGregor, his wife and one of their two children. They were face down between the structures.

After the fires died out, he scoured the property for clues but didn't find much. Their livestock wandered around with nowhere to go. He guessed at least eight horses left together by the number of hoofprints in the dirt by their gate. He wondered if the murderers were watching him. The lifespan of a sheriff was short, at best, unless you worked in a community of saints. He had yet to locate such a place.

He'd found an old shovel which had somehow escaped the fire and spent the last several hours digging through the charred rubble looking for the McGregor's other child. He kept asking himself who could do such a horrendous thing and why. The McGregor's were a loving couple who helped their neighbors. When he discovered the body, he had to walk away and empty his stomach. Whether it was the smoke, the physical exertion, the emotional stress, or the awful smell, Drake had given his all.

An eeriness settled over the farm like a dense fog. The sun peeked over the mountain range as if nothing had happened. Not one bird chirped, the animals were silent and what was once a nice farmhouse and barn were only black and gray smoldering piles. Everything had been taken from this family, including their lives.

Drake again sank his head under the icy water in the stream trying to wash the smoke away. It didn't help. He wanted to rid himself of the smell and sleep. If he could sleep. How would he put into words everything he'd seen, felt and heard? The silence of this morning had been deafening.

He'd tell Albert to round up the Undertaker and some men. After he slept, they'd bring back the bodies and bury them in the town cemetery. Blake filled his canteen, mounted his horse and took off toward Bozeman. The exhaustion he felt made it tough to stay in the saddle.

~

Drake woke to the sun shining through the window in the sheriff's office. He didn't remember how he got there. Gunner must've found his way back to town because the last thing he remembered was falling forward and wrapping his arms around his horse's neck.

Drake pushed himself up out of the cot and started a pot of coffee. The office door flung open.

"Hey boss, you're awake. I came by earlier and you were snoring loudly. I knew you'd been out all night, so I didn't want to wake you." Albert poured coffee into a cup and handed it to Drake.

"Albert, get the Undertaker and any men who will help. We have to go to the McGregor place. They were brutally murdered, their livestock is running loose, and their house and barn is burned to the ground." Drake took a gulp of coffee. It had never tasted so good. "Did you happen to tell Noel I am back?"

"Yes, I went to the bakeshop and told her you were here sleeping. You had passed out on the cot, with your face covered in soot and your clothes reeking of smoke. She came by about an hour later but since you were still asleep, she decided not to disturb you." Albert picked a plate up off his desk. "I have biscuits left from yesterday if you'd like one."

"I'll pass. I need to get a full meal in me. Thanks for telling Noel."

"She said Pastor Sheffield had rounded up some men to look for you. So I went by and told him you were back before they headed out. What happened up there?" Albert sat behind his desk.

"I'm guessing about eight outlaws shot the family and then set fire to the house and barn. It was pretty much gone by the time I got there. I happened to be on a hillside and saw smoke so I headed toward the fire. I didn't find any clues. I hope when we go back we'll find something which will lead us to these monsters." Drake finished the last drop of his coffee. "I'm gonna eat then head home to clean up. If you can round up help, I'll meet you here in two hours."

"I'm so angry at what those cold-blooded outlaws did. The McGregor's were good people. It won't be hard to find men who want to help." Albert followed Drake out of the office.

After visiting Mary's café and wolfing down his usual stack of pancakes, bacon, and eggs. Drake wanted to see his wife, so he stopped by the bakeshop. Eight people stood in line. He moved to the back of the bakeshop and waited for Noel to help each customer. Drake saw the bank owner, Charles Steele, following her every movement with his eyes. Steele hadn't seen him come in. Drake blended in with the customers and watched Noel wait on him. Her cheeks turned a light pink. Laughter and talking in the shop prevented him from hearing what Charles Steele said to her. Steele touched Noel's hand as she gave him change. *What's wrong with him? He knows we're married, and he evidently doesn't care.* Steele turned to leave and saw Drake. A smirk appeared on his face. Drake eyed him as he walked out the door. Oh, how he wanted to punch that smirk right off his face.

Drake figured his cover was blown, so he walked up to the counter. "You're busy." Noel's smile turned to a frown.

"I am. I stopped by the sheriff's office this morning but you were sleeping so I didn't wake you." Noel moved the pastries to the top shelf in the case.

"I'm sorry I didn't make it home last night. I saw smoke when I was up on the mountain, it turned out the McGregor's ranch was on fire. Someone burned down their house and barn and murdered the family. Nothing left by the time I got there. I spent most of the night looking for clues as to who might've done it and then rode back. I was so exhausted, I don't remember getting to the jail and falling asleep." Drake looked out the storefront window. Clouds were rolling in. "Since when did Steele start buying sweets here? Doesn't he employ a cook?"

"A few weeks ago. He comes in every couple of days. His cook doesn't like to bake she prefers to make meals. You can't save the world, Drake. You're only one man. You should've come to town first and got some men to ride out with you. Then told me, so I didn't have to wonder if you were all right. What if the murderers had still been there? They would've shot you too. Sometimes, I don't think you understand the worry those who care about you go through. So will you be home tonight?" Noel's eyes held a challenge he wanted to accept.

"I wish I could promise you that. A group of us are heading out to the McGregor's ranch to gather up the bodies and bring them to town. Albert and I will continue to search for evidence to help us find who committed this terrible crime. I hope to be back sometime tonight. By the way, I didn't like Steele touching your hand while you talked to him." Drake grabbed an apple muffin from a plate on the counter and Noel's face turned red.

"I don't think he meant anything by it. He's friendly to everyone. Now you're doing what I said you should've done in the first place. I won't wait up because you'll be late and I have to get up early to start baking."

"I doubt if he's that friendly with everyone. Steele is testing the waters to see what you might allow. I wouldn't expect you to stay up. I better go back to the office, looks like a storm is rolling in. Tell Steele to keep his hands off you in the future or I will pay him a visit and it won't be about taking out a loan."

"Really Drake, you're insulting me and acting like I'm a child! Mr. Steele couldn't care less about me and he knows we're married."

"I don't think it would stop a man like him." Bells jingled as Drake opened the door. He looked back but Noel ran into the kitchen. He wished he knew how to make her happy. He thought the bakeshop would keep her busy, and she'd understand the demands of his life better. But her disappointment in him was evident. She didn't grasp the responsibilities of his job.

As Drake walked to the jail, he saw the Undertaker and around ten men waiting for him out front. Drake wished he didn't have to go out to the McGregor's. The thought of those bodies made his stomach roll. He had to find their killers.

Snowflakes fell, landing on his shirt. It would be

a cold ride. Bozeman never lacked for snow during the winter and Drake never looked forward to the freezing temperatures outside or inside his home. He needed to balance his life and make things better with Noel. He loved her and didn't want to lose her.

Chapter Four

The sun's rays sent streaks of yellow light over the mountain tops and created a backdrop of gold behind the billowy white clouds floating in the sky. It snowed yesterday afternoon and most of the night. The sun reflected off the fresh snow and made gold sparkles glisten. Noel enjoyed the peacefulness of early morning and doing what she loved each day. She unlocked the door to the bakeshop, stepped inside and locked it behind her.

She expected a busy day; she had to bake more than yesterday. She always made the bread dough first so it would have time to rise and cinnamon rolls were a big seller. The aroma of butter and cinnamon baking helped her believe everything could be made right in the world. Smelling the dough frying for donuts caused her stomach to rumble in anticipation.

Noel had decorated the bakeshop in yellows, blues and greens to make everyone feel happy when they came to buy a treat. She wouldn't be sleeping much before Thanksgiving because of the many orders. It's a good thing she loved baking.

Drake had made it home about two in the morning. She heard him downstairs in the kitchen and assumed he was getting something to eat. When Noel went down the next morning, he'd been asleep on the sofa. Only embers remained in the hearth so she stirred them and put wood on top of the now red-hot coals. She missed having him next to her each night. She didn't know if she had the energy to make their marriage better.

A middle-aged woman knocked on the locked door. Noel could see her arms were full of boxes.

"Mildred! How are you today?" Noel asked as she opened the door and grabbed the top box.

"It's a beautiful morning and I'm blessed to be able to bring supplies for your bakeshop, so I'd say, doing just fine." Mildred smiled as she followed her to the kitchen.

"These eggs are so big, and the butter looks wonderful. My baking wouldn't be half as good without your delicious contributions. I'm so glad I don't have to rely on Sam's Mercantile for my eggs, butter, and milk all year long. The fruits, berries, vegetables, and cheese you delivered this past summer saved me lots of time and money. I've used all the pumpkins and apples you brought last week, so I'll want more for tomorrow." Noel set her box on the counter. "Sam's isn't known for keeping things in stock. It's hard enough to get sugar, flour and dry ingredients from him. I always try to order ahead so I have extra."

"I've always believed our farm products are the best." Mildred sat in a chair by the window. "Looks like you're baking more than usual today."

"I am. Yesterday was busy, I almost ran out. It's because Thanksgiving is only a couple of weeks away. I'm getting orders ahead of time. I'll probably be hiring someone to help me at least through Christmas. Have you heard of anyone who wants a job?" Noel brought a cup of coffee for Mildred and herself and two donuts then sat in the chair. Noel always looked forward to Mildred's deliveries and enjoyed their talks. She missed her mother, and Mildred was around her mother's age. It eased the homesickness Noel often had.

"I knew it'd only be a matter of time before word spread of your wondrous sweets. You've only been open six months and look at how busy you are. I don't know of anyone wanting a job, dear, but if I do, I'll send them your way." Mildred took a bite of her apple donut. "The icing is delicious. How's Drake doing? I couldn't believe it when I heard the McGregor's were murdered. So terrible! The life of a sheriff is hard."

"He hasn't been home so I haven't talked with him about it. He didn't get back until around two this morning." Noel didn't want to tell her he'd been sleeping on the sofa.

"The McGregor's were shot multiple times and the whole place burned to ashes. My son, Ben, rode out with them yesterday. He said it smelled awful, and he'd never forget how hard it had been to see the McGregor's. They didn't find any evidence that would lead them to who did it.

"Ben drove me into town today because he didn't want me coming in alone. My daughter-in-law, Deborah, and granddaughter, Chloe, came too so no one would be at the farm by themselves. We're considering hiring someone who will help with the chores and keep watch when we leave. Even though our farm is only a short distance from here, you can never be too safe." Mildred patted Noel's hand.

Noel couldn't think of anything to say. She hadn't thought that whoever had killed the McGregor's might try hurting someone in town. She should've, but it had not crossed her mind. She needed to be aware of what other people were going through, not just herself.

"I better finish my baking but you're more than welcome to come in the kitchen." Noel gathered up the dirty dishes and Mildred followed her. They talked until Noel unlocked the door.

The Pastor's wife, Alma Sheffield, and her six children stood outside waiting. It was a few minutes past opening time.

"Hello, Mrs. Sheffield. What can I get for you today?" Noel made her way behind the counter as they admired the sweets through the glass cases.

"Please Noel, call me Alma. We've known each other for a couple of years and your husband saved our daughter, Emma's life. We could never repay him. We consider Sheriff Drake and you part of our family and we hope you both feel the same about us." Alma smiled at Noel. "We came in for a special treat. It's my oldest son, Michael's birthday today, and he wanted donuts from his favorite baker."

Noel was uneasy around the pastor's wife. She was nice but Noel wondered if she secretly judged her. "How sweet of you, Michael."

Michael smiled as he gazed into the glass case full of cakes, donuts, and pastries while his little sister pulled on his shirt-tail.

"What kind of donuts would you like? I have more in the back if you don't see anything out here." Noel pulled another tray from the rack behind her.

"Do you have any with maple frosting?" Michael pointed to the far side of the glass case. "Are those chocolate ones?"

"Yes, you're right on both accounts." Noel put a half dozen of each flavor in a box plus an extra one for, Michael, since it was his birthday. Alma wanted to order a cake for her second to youngest child, John. His birthday was next month. They had planned to stop at five children, but three years ago, she had Sarah.

The sound level in the bakeshop increased as the younger children grew restless. The two oldest, Mary and Emma, tried to settle the little ones, but they refused to listen to them. Anxiety built up inside Noel. She didn't understand how three small children made such a ruckus. Noel's childhood had been quiet. Being an only child she had no one to fight or compete with. She'd always wanted a brother or sister, but as she got older, she liked not having to share.

Drake had saved their daughter, Emma's life after she'd waded into a creek at a church potluck and a wall of water came rushing toward her. It had been raining hard earlier in the day. The other children had left the water when their parents yelled, "Time to eat." Emma was making her way back to the bank as the water roared down the creek. When Drake heard the thunderous sound coming toward them he ran in, grabbed Emma and ran out. The rushing water swept by. His quick reactions saved her life, and everyone was amazed he got to her in time.

Emma was visibly shaken and ran to her mother sobbing. Drake's heroics were the talk of the town for the rest of the afternoon. He didn't relish the attention, but Noel noticed he appreciated it. She'd never contemplated how her life would be now, had Drake and Emma been swept away by the flash flood. Noel would be back in Denver going to parties and social gatherings with her parents. The thought of that sounded awful. She enjoyed working at her own bakeshop. She felt important and valued. She just wished her marriage gave her the same feeling.

Alma managed to herd up her children and thanked Noel as they left.

"I'm sorry Mildred, it took a while to take care of them. How does she manage so many children?" Noel sat down to her cold coffee and the half-eaten scone. "I would hide in my room afraid to come out."

"You do what you have to with what the good Lord blesses you with. If you did happen to get pregnant, Noel, once you held the baby in your arms you'd realize what a blessing they are." Mildred closed her eyes, lost in her memories.

"When I snuggled Ben for the first time, I cried tears of joy."

The door opened, and a young boy came in, his face dirty and his nose running. The hem on his pants was above his ankles and his filthy shirt wasn't long enough to cover his belly. He walked around the store. His eyes wide as he surveyed the sweets.

Noel hoped he'd keep his hands off the baked items she had out. What would other customers think if they saw him touching them?

Mildred walked over to him. "Hello son, what can we help you with today?"

"My mother is sick and we have no food." The boy wiped his runny nose on his sleeve. "She had my baby sister a couple of days ago but she cries all the time."

Noel walked over and whispered to Mildred. "Won't the church help them if they ask?"

"I'm not sure what they're capable of doing. They help a lot of people already." Mildred patted the blonde-haired boy on the head. "If you picked out your favorite sweet, what would it be?"

Why had Mildred asked him to pick out a sweet? She didn't want to get sick from him staying in the store. She'd have to give him something now or he wouldn't leave.

"A loaf of bread so my mom can share it with me."

Noel walked over to the counter. She might as well get the loaf of bread wrapped. "What's your name?"

"Andrew."

Mildred took his hand in hers. "Would you take me to your mother and sister?"

"Yes, ma'am. It's not far." Andrew looked up at Mildred.

"Good! Noel, please wrap that bread up and some donuts too." Mildred walked to the counter. "Put it on my tab and I'll pay for it tomorrow."

Noel boxed everything up and handed it to Mildred. "Be careful who you let stay on your farm. I wouldn't want anyone to cause trouble for you."

"Me neither, but we can't let these people starve. Someone has to care for them and see they have food." Mildred took the boy's hand again. "Andrew, let's find my son Ben and his family, and then we'll get your mother and baby sister and take them out to my farm. We have lots of room there and plenty to eat. Sounds like your mother needs that the most."

As Mildred and the boy left the bakeshop, Noel hoped she understood what she had committed to. Noel would never take someone home she didn't know, especially someone so sick they'd send their young son to beg for food.

"Thank you, Noel," Mildred called over her shoulder. "See you tomorrow morning."

Chapter Five

Drum beats echoed through Drake's head as he watched the beautifully dressed Crow Indian dancers. Kitchi invited him to their hunting ceremony a few weeks ago. The bison roamed the valleys in large herds this year and the tribe had an abundance of meat to dry.

The full moon bathed the area in a soft white glow while the bonfire shot sparks into the night sky eight to ten feet high. Drake's eyelids grew heavy.

Kitchi jabbed him in the side. "Not time to sleep."

"I'm trying to stay awake but I haven't slept much the last few days." Drake stretched. The Crow had only allowed him to see two of their ceremonies. Even though they were at peace with the white man, Drake sensed their distrust, and he couldn't blame them. The white man promised land then took it back.

Drake had only been home a few hours this week. It took time to investigate the murders and fire at the McGregor ranch. They still didn't have any suspects.

He valued Kitchi's friendship, but he needed to go home. The drums stopped, and Drake realized the dance had ended. He looked at Kitchi. "I should leave."

Hurit, Kitchi's sister walked toward them. "Did you like dance?" She smiled.

"Yes." He'd never paid attention before, but Hurit was a beautiful young woman. He wondered what handsome brave had his eye on her.

Hurit grabbed her brother's arm. "Let's eat."

Kitchi spoke to her in Crow and Hurit hurried off.

"What did you say?"

"I told her bring furs. You leaving."

Drake untied Gunner from a tree. Hurit ran back and handed him the furs. They would be warm if he stopped and slept for a few hours.

"Thank you, Kitchi."

"You stay here?" Kitchi motioned toward the fire in the middle of camp.

"Not many in your tribe would want me to stay. They don't trust me like you, Kitchi." Drake mounted Gunner.

"Ride strong. Be brave." Kitchi smacked Gunner on the rump.

Drake waved as they galloped into the night. Weariness settled on his shoulders. He should've stayed in town. Maybe, Noel had a few valid points. He wanted to do everything everyone expected of him and it wasn't possible. Other things suffered from his lack of attention, mainly, his wife. She didn't understand his responsibility to the townspeople.

He shouldn't be riding alone at night when he was this tired and there were murderers about. He'd made it halfway to town when he couldn't stay awake, so he stopped and built a fire to get a couple of hours of sleep.

He laid the furs out by the fire, took his boots off and crawled in between them. The odor from the bearskin bothered him, at first, but he soon forgot about it and slept. He dreamt of being home with Noel.

~

Drake opened the door to the bakeshop. The aroma of fresh baked bread and cinnamon greeted him. *Could it get any better?* He had the place to himself, the morning crowd must be gone.

"You stink." Noel walked from behind the glass cases and stood in front of him sniffing.

"Probably the furs I slept on last night. Kitchi gave me a couple, so I could sleep without freezing. The odor bothered me but I went to sleep so fast I forgot about it." Drake wanted to touch the curl that fell alongside her face. "I just returned."

"You need a bath. Why were you with the Crow Indians? It's anywhere but home anymore, isn't it?" Noel's brown eyes accused him of not loving her.

"It isn't like that. I want to be with you but I need their trust too. I spent most of my time this week looking for the McGregor's killers. I don't want anyone else to be murdered."

"You have a home but you're never there. You have a wife but you don't have time for her. When I agreed to move to Montana, I didn't want to be here alone. I should've stayed in Denver." Noel walked back behind the counter. "You're making the whole place stink. No one will buy anything now."

Drake caught movement from the corner of his eye. A couple was opening the bakeshop door. "I'm leaving." He waited until they came in before he walked out. He went home to heat water for a bath. No need to make anyone else suffer today. He'd wanted to surprise Noel, instead, he made her even more upset. Drake wondered why Kitchi never stunk as bad as he did.

Maggie and Tucker greeted him at the back door and then ran into the sitting room. *Even the dogs don't like my new scent.* He pulled the metal tub into the kitchen and boiled pots full of water to fill it.

~

Drake threw wood in the stove and watched the flames flicker and then take off. He sat in his chair as the jail heated up. His eyelids closed, and he dozed off for a few minutes. He woke with a start as something ran over his hand. A mouse hurried across the desk and down one of the table legs. The jail cells were empty, so he put his black duster on and stepped outside. It was his night to make sure law was upheld in Bozeman.

Cold air hit him the moment he stepped out the door. A half-moon didn't give much light as music from the saloons mixed together in a disjointed noise. Truth be told, he preferred the animals in the wilderness over the animals hiding behind the doors of those establishments.

Word had gotten out that the Sheriff of Bozeman didn't tolerate public drunkenness, but that never stopped the ones who needed to find out for themselves. If not for the drifters, Bozeman would be a pretty quiet place to live.

Drunkenness, gambling and womanizing were the biggest causes of fights. The saloons were where most of them started but the brothels had their share. As Sheriff, Drake dealt with the worst of humanity. When people were raised without a sense of what was morally right, they became animals.

Drake detoured down a side street so he could walk the alley. The saloons closed around two in the morning so most of the men would be home by now. If he found anyone passed out they'd get a free night in a jail cell to sober up.

He thought of the conversation with Noel and how she accused him of not wanting to be home. The men who stayed in the saloons until two didn't want to be home, not him. He wanted to be with Noel so bad he felt it in every fiber of his being. Drake had been hired to do a job, and it required a lot. He shouldn't have married until he'd gotten over the desire to be a sheriff. It hadn't been fair to his wife.

A door opened down the dark alleyway. A man ventured out and walked away from him. Drake followed him. He'd exited from the back of one of the finer brothels in town if you could use the word "finer" for a brothel of ill-repute.

Madam Susie ran a tight ship. Her girls weren't allowed in public. She hired errand boys to buy what they needed. She took them into the country in a covered wagon on Sunday mornings so they could enjoy the fresh air. The rest of the time they stayed within the four walls of the brothel.

The word around town amongst the men who frequented these dens of desire was Madam Susie shouldn't be crossed. Occasionally, one of these ladies of the evening might be dismissed from her working duties. Madam Susie had her on a train to somewhere or possibly nowhere the next morning.

Drake kept his distance from the man in front of him so he wouldn't be heard. He strolled down the back streets and alleys. He didn't want to be seen. He might be married.

When they reached the west part of town, Drake realized who he was and it didn't surprise him, Charles Steele. The same man trying to garner Noel's favor at the bakeshop. None other than the upstanding owner of the only bank in Bozeman and the supposed desire of all the single women.

Drake never believed he was the man he pretended to be. He attended church every Sunday while the women fawned over him. Steele looked and played the part of the perfect gentleman and upstanding citizen but he obviously had another side few knew about.

Drake watched him go through his door and then he walked back toward town. So why Noel? Maybe the challenge of winning the affection of a married woman added another level of enticement. Steele could marry any single lady in Bozeman but yet he wanted to pay for his pleasures.

If Steele had secrets, he had an agenda for doing so. Out of the seven dens of iniquity lining the red-light district in Bozeman, there had to be a reason he visited Madam Susie's. Maybe because of the way she kept her "ladies" from the public? Drake decided to make spying on Steele a priority. He walked back to the sheriff's office. His instincts had proven right again.

The fire had warmed up the jail nicely while he'd been gone. He brewed a pot of coffee, pulled out a pencil and paper and recorded everything he knew about Steele. Tomorrow Drake would make inquiries, but tonight he'd found new motivation to keep him awake.

Voices shouting erupted outside. He shoved the paper and pencil back in the drawer and took the coffee pot off the stove. Time to restore the peace.

Chapter Six

Noel pulled back on the horse's reins, the wagon stopped in front of a light-yellow farmhouse. Roses grew along the porch in every color. Vines climbed up the corner posts and a huge tree shaded both the porch and lawn. Mildred's home looked charming.

Noel jumped down and reached into the back of the wagon grabbing the handle of a big pot. It was heavy and awkward to lift out. She walked up the porch steps and tapped on the door.

Andrew opened the front door.

"Hello, Andrew! I came to visit Mrs. Mayfield." Noel couldn't believe the change in the boy.

"I'll tell, Mr. Mayfield, you're here."

"Thank you, Andrew. I brought soup. My mother always gave me chicken noodle soup when I had a stomachache or cold."

Andrew ran down the porch stairs toward the barn yelling. "Mr. Mayfield, the bake lady is here!"

A woman holding a baby came to the door. "Hello, my name is Catherine. I'm Andrew's mother. I heard you ask for Mildred."

"Yes. Hello Catherine, I'm Noel West. Mildred delivers supplies to my bakeshop. Her son, Ben, came to the shop yesterday and told me she wasn't doing well, so I made her some chicken soup."

"How nice of you. Mildred took a nap so she'll be ready to eat and I'm sure will enjoy a visit."

"Thank you. I'll only stay for a bit. How are you adjusting to living here?"

"It's been such a blessing. I'd lost all hope after my Jimmy died and then Lily came, and I got so sick. We would have been in a bad place if Mildred hadn't asked us to stay here. I've enjoyed helping her and Andrew loves the farm." Catherine bounced Lily as she started to fuss.

"I'm glad you found a safe place to stay." Noel looked at her shoes. A voice boomed from behind her and she jumped.

"Does your husband know you came here alone? He's been telling everyone to take someone with them if they go anywhere." Ben held out his hand. "Let me carry the soup in for you?" Ben took the soup pot and walked through the door.

Noel followed. "No, I didn't get a chance to tell him. I forgot about the murderers who haven't been caught. I wanted to visit Mildred, she's always so helpful to everyone."

"Yeah, since the McGregor's were murdered, and their ranch burned to the ground, whoever did it might be waiting to attack someone else. I'd go back to town with you, but it would leave the women here alone. You should keep the visit short so you won't be going home close to dark."

How insulting. The man had no tact.

"Mother's room is on the right. Just knock before you go in."

Noel smoldered. *Doesn't he think I have enough sense to knock before going in?* She brought food for the family and now she regretted it. "Thank you, I'll be sure to knock first." If Ben didn't want to leave everyone alone then why did he make deliveries yesterday for his mother? Oh well, she made it out here without trouble, so Noel trusted she'd return the same.

Noel tapped on Mildred's door.

"Who is it?" Mildred's voice sounded less than normal.

"It's me, Noel. I brought you some chicken soup and wanted to see how you're doing."

"Come in."

Noel entered the room and sat in a floral covered chair next to the bed. Mildred looked pale except for spots of pink on her cheeks. "Are you running a temperature?"

"Yes, I've been drinking Doctor Brown's prescribed tea. My whole body aches and I feel useless lying in this bed." Mildred coughed.

"Your body is telling you to rest. Let other people care for you. You've more than earned it." Noel squeezed Mildred's hand.

"I suppose you're right, dear, but it's not easy to be idle."

Noel adjusted Mildred's quilt. "You'll be up in no time. I'm glad you have Catherine here to help.

She probably stays busy with Andrew and the baby though."

"Catherine's a great help to me. The good Lord knew when to send them into my life. Here I thought I'd be helping them but turns out, she's been helping me. Ben's wife, Deborah, is so busy with her four little ones, she isn't able to do much here."

"I'm glad you didn't listen to me when I told you not to take them in. I judged Catherine by the way Andrew looked but she couldn't help it. I assumed she might be lazy, but she isn't." Noel looked down.

"You're being too hard on yourself. We all misjudge people. To be honest, I didn't want to bring them home either, but God kept tugging at my heart and I had to obey. Ben wouldn't talk to me for two days because he got so mad. But after seeing how Catherine works, he realized he'd misjudged her too. Would you hand me my cup of water from the table?"

Noel handed her the cup. "I'm glad things worked out for everyone. Sometimes, I act like my mother, thinking I'm above others who are less fortunate than I am. But, I'm no better than Catherine. If her husband hadn't died, she wouldn't have been left in such distress. I cringe when I remember my thoughts toward Andrew. You were their angel here on earth."

Mildred handed her water back to Noel. "The good book tells us to love our neighbor as ourselves. We all can do it, but fear of the unknown keeps us from acting."

"You're right. I need to think of others more." Noel stood up. "I should head back to town before it gets dark."

"You came out here alone? Where's that sheriff husband of yours?"

"I didn't tell him I was coming."

"Well, you get Ben to ride back to town with you. You need to inform that fine man of yours where you're off to next time. He'll worry himself sick."

"Sometimes I wonder how many days it would take him to notice I'm not there."

"Noel, honey, that's not true. Your man loves you the same as my late husband loved me. He may be busy being sheriff but his thoughts are all about you. I wish the Mayor would hire more deputies. It's been hard on him."

"You're probably right, but it's hard being alone." Noel hugged Mildred. "Get better and I hope you enjoy the soup."

"Thank you, Noel. I'm sure it's delicious like everything you make. Don't forget to tell Ben I want him to ride back into town with you."

Noel nodded her head as she closed the door. She didn't plan on speaking to Ben about anything after he'd made it clear she'd be going back alone. Besides, it only took thirty minutes to get to town from here.

~

The outskirts of town came into view just as Noel heard a thundering noise behind her. She looked back and a cloud of dust grew bigger as it got closer. She snapped the reins to get the horses moving faster. All the talk of outlaws had her spooked.

Normally, she rode Ruby, but she couldn't because she had the pot of soup to bring. No one could catch her that far out on Ruby, although, in this wagon, they most likely would before she got to town.

As she rounded a rock formation, a rider raced toward her. When had this route become so traveled? She hoped it would be someone she knew. As they got closer to each other, she realized it was Drake. She'd never been happier to see his face.

"What are you doing out here alone?" He yelled as he turned his horse to ride alongside the wagon and keep their hurried pace toward town.

Her happy thoughts diminished at the tone of his voice. "I took Mildred some soup, she's been sick."

"The outlaws who killed the McGregor's are still roaming free."

"Did you notice the dust cloud?"

"Yes, that's why I rode Gunner so hard to get to you. Violet told me you'd left to visit Mildred alone."

"I'm sorry, Drake. I should've told you but you're never around."

"I'm thankful you're all right. Please don't go anywhere alone. Everyone needs to be cautious until we find the murderers. I need to tell Ben and the other ranchers they might want to hire more men to ensure the safety of their families and property."

"Has there been any other crimes since the McGregor murders?"

"No."

They were back in town now, and Drake waved at Pastor Sheffield as they made their way down the street.

People probably wondered why Drake rode so hard out of town and then came back a short time later escorting her in a wagon. Let them make up their own stories, she wouldn't satisfy their curiosity.

Drake jumped off Gunner and unhitched the horses from the wagon when they stopped by the stable.

"Why don't we go to the restaurant at the hotel tonight? I'm sure you're tired after all the excitement and Albert's on duty."

"I'd have to freshen up. I look like a dust cloud."

"Take your time, I have to brush down the horses, feed and water them, then clean up myself."

Noel opened the stable door. Drake walked the horses inside. "It's been so long since we've had dinner together. It will be like when we were courting."

"I miss being able to do things with you."

Drake's words made her smile. There might still be something between them? She loved Drake. She walked back to the house remembering their first years together.

When she got upstairs, she opened her dresser. Noel wanted to find the necklace Drake gave her when they were courting. As she reached into the drawer her hand touched paper. It was wrapped around the red glass heart. She never asked Drake if it had been him who left it. She worried what he'd say if it wasn't. She searched the other side of the drawer and found the gold heart with a pearl in the middle. She hadn't worn it in years. She wondered if he'd remember.

Noel washed up and picked out her favorite gown. Her mother had bought it for her before they moved. She'd only wore it a couple of times, as there weren't many occasions to wear it to in Bozeman.

The dress was made of brown taffeta with burgundy accents on the sides of the skirt. Rows of ruffles made the back of the skirt a work of art. Her thoughts drifted back in time through the special nights Drake and she had spent together. Her anticipation grew as she wanted her husband to notice the details she went through to prepare for their dinner. Noel might be overdressed, but she wanted to look nice for Drake.

When she walked downstairs, the room was empty. Had Drake left? What reason would it be this time?

The back door closed, and her handsome sheriff walked into the room. His eyes met hers and she couldn't look away.

"You look beautiful, Noel. Even more beautiful than the day I gave you this necklace." Drake crossed the room and his fingers touched her skin as he took the gold heart between them.

His touch caused warmth to run through her body. *He has to realize how much I love him.* She wondered if he'd kiss her, part of her wanted him to, but he let the heart slip from his fingers and took a step back.

"Shall we go?"

Noel tried to find her voice, but it came in a whisper. "Yes."

Chapter Seven

Drake eased back in the saddle as he galloped toward town. He'd been talking with ranchers the last few days to ask if any strangers had passed through. Most of them hadn't seen anyone. A few ranch hands said some men rode through the outskirts of their land when they'd been out driving cattle. They didn't try to stop them, but they kept an eye on them.

He needed to go to the mayor and ask for a couple more deputies. A deputy to ride with him and one to help Albert in town. Although, even two against a gang of outlaws didn't stand a chance.

Gunner had been getting too much exercise and Drake grew weary from the long days and nights. He didn't feel at ease riding through the tall grass in the valley or the tree-crowded forests. He might be ambushed, and it wouldn't end well.

A cold clear stream awaited him farther up the trail. Both Gunner and he wanted to rest and drink some water to quench their thirst. Drake slid off his horse and led him to the creek bank where they drank side by side. He owed this horse for his faithful companionship, no one else spent as much time with him as Gunner did.

A noise alerted Drake, and he pulled his gun from the holster. It sounded as if someone was in pain. *Why would anyone be out here?* He stood, trying not to make any noise. He hoped Gunner stayed quiet. Again, he heard moaning and cautiously headed toward it. As he drew closer to the sounds, he crouched down and looked for movement.

The chirping bird and gurgling creek covered the sound of his racing heart. He inched forward and saw someone lying on the ground in the dense undergrowth ahead of him. He cocked his gun as he moved closer. Drake recognized the clothing as the type the Crow Indian women wore. This woman he wasn't moving. It might be a trap. He had to be alert.

He pushed through the bushes near her and she remained motionless. He knelt beside her and watched her chest rise and fall. Blood had dried on her face from a deep cut on her forehead. She looked familiar. As he wiped the blood off, he realized it was Hurit, Kitchi's sister. Her dress had been ripped in multiple places. She had bruises and cuts over her arms, face, and legs. He could tell she tried to fight back against her attackers. He feared they'd raped her.

Drake gently shook her shoulders and said her name, but only a small sound escaped her lips. He had to get her back to Kitchi and her parents. He picked Hurit up and carried her to Gunner. He laid her over the front part of the saddle, keeping her there as he pulled himself up. He gathered her against him, her head laid against his chest, while he held her close. Drake pushed Gunner into a fast trot. They headed toward the Crow camp. She didn't look good. He hoped whoever attacked her, wouldn't be waiting to surprise him and finish them both off.

The sun was setting behind the mountains when Drake rode into the Indian camp.

Braves and squaws came out of their teepees. When the Crow Indians noticed Hurit the women started screaming. The Braves pulled Hurit from his grasp and carried her to the medicine man's tent. They drug Drake off Gunner and pushed him face first to the ground and then tied his hands behind his back. After talking amongst themselves, they took him into a teepee and left him there. Drake wondered why he had not seen Kitchi.

~

Cold air hit him in the face as the flap to the teepee opened. He must have dozed off for a while. Kitchi walked in.

He stared at Drake. "You did this?"

"How can you ask me that? I would never harm any woman." Drake recognized hurt in his friend's eyes. Sorrow fell like a mantle upon his shoulders and Kitchi slumped forward. *Why would he believe this of me?* Drake understood then how thin the line of trust between them ran even though Kitchi had saved his life.

"I not believe you hurt her, had to hear you speak it." Kitchi untied Drake.

"Who believes I did this?" Drake tried to rub the numbness out of his hands.

Kitchi brought a bucket of water to Drake. "Some do, most do not. They don't think you bring her back if you did."

"I found her in the forest. No one else was around." Drake took a sip from the ladle. "I heard her moaning when I got a drink from the creek. I brought her back as fast as I could. Is she all right?"

"She not awake. Someone hurt her badly. I will kill them." Kitchi picked up an ax and threw it at one of the poles holding up the tent. It met its mark.

"I understand your anger, but I don't want you to hang for murder. If you find them, let me take them in. They will pay for what they've done. It might be the same men who killed the McGregor's and burned down their ranch."

"White man's justice not good for us. Yesterday she hunt. My father told her not go alone. She not return, I went searching. I not here when you come, still looking." Kitchi walked over to the tent flap and looked out.

Drake stood up. "I'm sorry, my friend. Whoever is responsible will be brought to justice. I promise you I won't stop searching until I find them. I need to head back. Let me know how Hurit is doing?"

~

Drake pulled his duster tighter as he shivered uncontrollably in the dark alleyway. Every night he was on duty, he'd wait in the shadows, to observe if Steele visited Madam Suzie's Brothel. In the last couple of weeks, Drake had seen him leave three times.

Two nights ago after Steele left, one of the girls came out to smoke. Drake tried to approach her, but she hurried back inside.

Steele took the same path through the alley every time. Drake wondered if he'd be in the front pew as usual on Sunday. How did a man lead one type of life in the daytime and a completely different one at night? Didn't his conscious bother him? Drake considered the men who looked you in the eye and shook your hand then stabbed you in the back the most dangerous.

The door to Madam Suzie's opened. "Get the Doc, she's hurt bad." A half-dressed woman ran down the alley.

Drake kept his distance and followed her to Doc Bradford's, where she banged frantically on the door until he opened it.

"We need you quick, Doc! Della was beaten badly." The woman waited outside while Doc Bradford went back in.

He came out with his coat and bag and they hurried back to the brothel while Drake kept them in his sight. Drake would make his presence known and find out what happened to Della. He hoped one of the girls would talk. The madam of a house of ill-repute never called the sheriff about anything, unless someone died.

Secrecy in their line of business was key to their customer's trust. They'd rather a girl be roughed around a bit than lose a customer. It didn't matter whether it was a low-class saloon or a so-called, high-class brothel, like Madam Suzie's. The girls were replaceable the loss of income not.

Drake grabbed the Doc's arm as he opened the back door to Madam Susie's.

"I've been following you both. I overheard her say one of the girls was beaten. I need to find out how bad she's hurt. If someone is hitting women, they'll be arrested."

Doc Bradford scowled at Drake. "They don't tell me what goes on. I only treat the injuries."

The rumors must be true. The prostitution bosses were paying him off to keep quiet. "If someone were to die, and you didn't report their injuries to me, I'd put you in jail and charge you as an accomplice. You better make sure you don't take your silence too far." Drake held the door open as the doctor tried to shut it behind him.

"You have too much time on your hands, Sheriff. You're wasting it hanging out in back alleys. Doc Bradford sneered at Drake. Do you have your eye on one of the ladies?"

Drake clenched his fists. He wanted to punch him in the face. He didn't become a doctor to help the sick and hurting. The money meant more to him than any lives, especially those he judged unworthy of compassion.

"I'm coming with you." Drake pushed past the woman in the doorway. "Come in if you must Sheriff, but Madam Suzie ain't going to like it."

"I'm not usually liked when I show up." Drake followed them up the back stairs.

The room was lit by one candle. Madam Suzie stood at the head of the bed while another girl cleaned the cuts on Della's face and body.

"Tell me who did this?" Drake entered the room.

Madam Suzie looked at Doc and shook her head. "We're not sure."

"Of course. The answer I expected. You don't care if these women are beaten and abused. You only think about the men's reputations who pay you money to hurt the girls in your establishment." Drake stared at the Madam and Doc. "How the two of you sleep at night is beyond my understanding."

"There are many things beyond your understanding, Sheriff. Like, who killed that poor family and burnt their farm. Or how lonely your wife is. You should spend more time at home and less where it's none of your business." Madam Suzie walked past him toward the door. "I am through here. Let me know what you find out Doc Bradford."

"Of course." Doc smiled. "I'll need everyone to leave, so I can examine her."

Drake followed the girl who'd been cleaning Della's cuts. As they walked out of the room Drake whispered. "Do you know who did this?"

She looked around. "I might, but I can't say."

"Could you talk to me? Send a note to the jail and I'll meet you."

She nodded her head and hurried down the hall. Drake walked into the elaborately decorated front parlor of the brothel. He was struck by the gaudiness. Red velvet drapes covered every window while gold-painted chairs with black cushions sat around the room. A huge chandelier hung from the ceiling. A piano waited to be played. A couple of men waited for their turn with their favorite gal. Some girls as young as fifteen. When Drake went in they shielded their faces.

"One of the girls got hurt here tonight, gentlemen, so you might hurry home before you become a suspect. Find yourself a woman you can love and marry her. This ain't a good place to be. You're apt to catch some disease and die." Drake put his hand on his revolver.

Both men scurried out without a backward glance.

Madame Suzie walked into the room. He wondered why she came back. Her dress matched the gold and red upholstery on the chairs and curtains. "Why are you chasing my customers away?"

"If I had the authority, I'd shut you down tonight. Unfortunately, you have friends in high places. Just know I'll be watching you and every other sleazy place in this town." Drake walked to the door.

Madam Suzie fanned herself with a lace fan. "I'll be watching you too sheriff. Better make sure you don't get out of line or something might happen."

Drake turned around. "Is that a threat?"

"Of course not. I'd hate to hear anything happened to that pretty wife of yours. Rumor is she's home alone all the time. Who knows what type of person might want to experience what you've been missing out on." Madam Suzie laughed, and Drake realized evil stood before him in the shape of a woman.

"If anything ever happens to my wife, I will hunt you down and kill anyone who had any part in it."

"You can only do that if you're alive." Madam Susie glared at him with such intensity he didn't doubt she'd love to kill him right now.

"They can try." Drake slammed the door so hard, the vibration shook the ground under his feet. He'd just declared war on all the fine establishments in this town and word got around quickly. Drake better ask for more deputies tomorrow and make sure someone watched over Noel when he wasn't in Bozeman.

He looked up at the windows in the brothel and noticed the girl who agreed to meet him peeking out one of them from behind a curtain. He hoped to never know the hopelessness these women experienced. They were trapped in this prison until they died or Madam Suzie threw them out.

He walked to the jail, locked everything up and headed home. He wasn't going to stay there tonight. He had to make sure Noel would be safe.

When he got home, he walked inside and sat on the sofa in the cold dark house. It didn't seem like he belonged anymore. His life was falling apart and now he'd put his wife in danger. Maybe they should pack up and move back to Denver, it would be safer. But Drake knew he couldn't. He never backed down from threats, although, a time might come when he'd put Noel on a train headed to her parents. They'd be happy to tell Noel, "He turned out just as we predicted. A man who can't take care of his wife or keep her love."

Chapter Eight

Noel walked downstairs to the sound of Drake snoring. The quilt he'd covered himself with lay on the floor next to the sofa. It was the one she'd made for him when they were first married. The room was cold, no fire burned in their hearth. She put wood on the few glowing embers and waited for it to catch. After a few air blasts from the bellows, the fire roared into life. She picked up the quilt and laid it over him. She wondered why he hadn't stayed at the jail. Deputy Albert may have come back in.

She looked forward to closing the bakeshop tomorrow for Thanksgiving. Noel hoped they'd be able to spend it together without any emergencies. Violet was coming over for supper but the rest of the day they could enjoy alone. Their dinner at the hotel had been fun, but only a brief consolation, as she had been alone every night since.

Noel's emotions ran from hope to

discouragement each day concerning their marriage. She hadn't meant for him to spend every night on the sofa, but he took it as such. She had got upset one time because he woke her up coming in late. Noel rose with the sun to start baking so she had to go to bed early. She wondered why he didn't sleep in the guest room, it'd be more comfortable. Maybe he saw the sofa as temporary, and the guest room as permanent.

She forgot what it felt like to have a real marriage? Drake was married to his job more than to her. They had grown so far apart they rarely talked. They shared a house and pets but not much more. She loved him and understood the demands of being a sheriff. If Drake couldn't find time for her, though, he should've never asked her to be his wife.

Noel grabbed her coat and mittens and headed out into the frosty morning. Drake always took care of the horses. It had snowed, and a couple of inches remained on the ground. There would be two or three feet of snow before long. She'd bought a turkey from Mildred for Thanksgiving and planned on making all the sides; dressing, potatoes and gravy, and corn.

Today should be busy and she'd be working into the evening. Orders for Thanksgiving desserts and rolls had poured in over the last few days and she hoped she had enough supplies to fill them. She needed rolls and pies for their Thanksgiving dinner too.

Violet said she'd help today and Mary Sheffield, the oldest daughter of Pastor and Alma Sheffield, would be in to bake. Noel admired Mary's love for life and asked her to work at the shop when things got really busy. She turned sixteen in September and had been baking the last couple of days. She caught on fast and Noel was encouraged she had found the right helper. Violet only helped if Noel didn't have anyone else.

Thanksgiving tomorrow meant her favorite holiday, Christmas, would be here before she knew it. She loved Christmas. The tree filled their home with the scent of pine. Candles glowing through-out the house. Gifts wrapped and tied with pretty bows waiting to be opened. Smells of ham cooking in the oven.

There were a few times during the years she considered having children and Christmas was one of them. She'd love to see the happiness on her child's face Christmas morning. When Noel was little, she tried to stay awake Christmas Eve to hear Santa come down the chimney. She'd been lucky her parents never struggled financially so Christmas morning was a sight to behold. Presents covering the floor around the tree. New dresses and shoes, bows for her hair and at least one new doll to love.

She knew Christmas held more meaning than gifts and she'd heard the Christmas story many times. How Jesus came to earth as a baby to save us if we'd believe in Him. To Christians, it meant a lot, but to her, it was a nice story. Drake had agreed, but as he spent more time with the Sheffield's, his beliefs were changing. Mary might be able to help Noel understand why it meant so much to them.

She attended church a few times growing up,

Christmas and Easter. Her parents often told her the Bible was as real as her book of *Grimm's Fairy Tales*. They contained nice stories but were only make-believe.

Homesickness hit her as she thought of her father and mother, although, home would never be the same. Her father had divorced her mother. She assumed her parents would always be together, they'd looked so in love and rarely argued.

Drake's parents had been very poor. They worked hard on their farm but the weather determined how well their crops did. Drake was the oldest and helped his father from the time he was knee-high to a grasshopper, so the saying went. His younger sisters helped his mother with the garden and house. His sisters were married now and lived near his parents. Laura had two children and Amy three.

Drake's parents sent letters regularly asking if any grandchildren would be coming soon. The answer was always no, and Noel envisioned their disappointment as they read each letter. His parents had been married thirty-five years and Noel had looked up to the way they loved each other in action and deed. They were a team and family their first priority. She wondered what they'd think of Drake being gone so much.

Her thoughts kept her occupied all the way to the bakeshop. She unlocked the door and stepped inside. Time to get the stoves going and warm this place up. She turned around to lock the door but Mr. Steele pushed it open and walked in.

"We aren't open yet." Noel looked into his dark

blue eyes.

"I know, I'd hoped to find time alone with you." His eyes traveled down her body.

Noel stood frozen. Never had a man been so forward with her. Mr. Steele took hold of her hand and she gently tried to pull it free but he held onto it. His thumb caressed the top part of it. "I need to get to my baking." Noel pulled harder this time to free her hand. He let go. Mr. Steele was handsome with his black hair combed neatly back, he dressed every bit the wealthy banker. Impeccable, would be the word she'd use to describe his appearance.

"It can wait a few minutes. I want to place an order for tomorrow. I meant to do it yesterday, but it slipped my mind." He followed Noel to the counter where she took out a paper and pencil.

"What would you like?" Noel looked at him.

Mr. Steele smiled in such a way that Noel knew his thoughts were not on pies or rolls. An alarm sounded in her consciousness, but there was a charm about him that kept her mesmerized. It crossed her mind she might be playing with fire, but something in her craved to be desired again.

"If I answered your question truthfully, you might not let me back in here or you might find my answer worth exploring. I haven't figured you out, but I will. For now, let's just say, I'd like a cherry and apple pie and about two dozen rolls. I'm planning a dinner for a few of my employees. No one bakes as well as you do, Noel."

Noel caught her breath with his use of her first name. She was a married woman, and he was crossing all sorts of boundaries. She needed to stop him, but instead, she just stared into his eyes, unable to say anything. The tension between them became as thick as mud after the snow melted. He reached across the counter and brushed a loose strand of hair away from her eyes, his fingers touching her face.

The bell on the door jingled and Noel jumped. Mr. Steele moved his hand back.

"Boy, it's cold outside." Violet walked in. "You haven't gotten the stoves going yet?"

"It's my fault. I've distracted her with an order for Thanksgiving. I hadn't noticed the cold. When will it be ready, Mrs. West?" Mr. Steele smiled at Violet.

"Later this afternoon." Noel wrote down what he wanted.

"Great, I'll be back then. Good day, ladies." Mr. Steele walked out the door and Noel released her breath, unaware she'd been holding it.

"What was going on, Noel?" Violet walked over in front of her. "It looked like he might kiss you across the counter when I came in. Do I have to remind you, you're a married woman? If it had been anyone other than me who'd just witnessed what I did, talk would be all over town about you cheating on your husband! Can you imagine how hurt Drake would be?"

"Mr. Steele took me by surprise. I had just opened the door and walked inside. I turned around to lock it when he pushed it open and came in, almost as if he'd been waiting for me. He kept looking at me and I felt confused. I wanted to move away from him but my feet were glued to the floor. I'm so glad you came in, Violet, your timing was perfect." Noel went to the kitchen.

"I won't always be here to save you from yourself. You need to realize what you are jeopardizing and for what? Once Mr. Steele got from you what he wanted, he'd go on to his next victim? It's the quest which gives him pleasure. I've been around men like him before. Don't get me wrong, Noel, you're a beautiful woman but Mr. Steele could marry any single lady in town. Why else would he choose you if not for the conquest? Or a vendetta against Drake. Be careful, he's a powerful man." Violet followed her into the kitchen. "Well, that was an interesting start to my morning. Personally, Noel, that man gives me the creeps."

Chapter Nine

Drake knocked on Pastor Sheffield's door. He hadn't talked with him for a few months. He wanted advice on how to fix his marriage. Emma opened their door and gave him a hug. Since Drake had saved her life, they'd been good friends.

He followed her into Pastor Sheffield's study. Books lined the wall in back of the Pastor's desk. Drake wondered if he'd read them all.

"Have a seat Drake. It's good to see you. Probably been a couple of months since we talked, wouldn't you say? I hear you've been busier than ever."

Drake mumbled, "Yeah, that's part of my problem."

"Sure glad we didn't have to search for you when the McGregor's place burnt to the ground. You know, we were very worried where you were that day, especially Mrs. West. You should tell her where you're going.

I'm sure you know Mary started working for your wife. Today is her third day, and she loves it. With Thanksgiving tomorrow, Mary said they have more orders than they may be able to fill. It will be a late night. What brings you here other than enjoying my company?" Pastor Sheffield chuckled at his own joke.

"Noel didn't tell me Mary went to work at the bakeshop. It's good she has help. We don't talk much and you're right, I should let her know where I am whenever possible. I want to make my marriage better. Noel doesn't understand my long hours and commitments. She accuses me of not wanting to be with her, which couldn't be farther from the truth." Drake sat back in his chair. "I've slept on the sofa for a few months now. Everything I say is wrong. I hoped our marriage would be so much happier. I love her."

"I'm sorry, Drake, I had no idea. I understand, probably as well as anyone, how being at everyone's beck and call during a crisis can strain a marriage. You are summoned at any time to help."

"I'm afraid I didn't anticipate how great the need would be and how much time it would consume when I took the job. I always wanted to be a lawman, but now I understand why most never marry. If I don't stop being sheriff, it won't get better. And if I quit the only other work I know is ranching, but it wouldn't support us in the way Noel is accustomed to."

Drake glanced out the window. Snowflakes floated downward, it seemed so peaceful when you were inside a warm house. "Her parents are wealthy, and she had the best of everything growing up. I haven't provided that kind of life for her, but we have a nice home and what we need." Pastor Sheffield had been writing a few notes and Drake wondered if they were about him.

"Can you cut down the time you're away? Could your deputy do the traveling?"

"I would want another deputy to stay in Bozeman while I taught Albert. I'd have to introduce him to the Crow and the ranchers who aren't in town much. I couldn't send him out without preparing him for what he might face." Drake got up and paced in front of the window.

"I understand the dilemma you're in. Why don't you approach the mayor and ask if he might agree to add another deputy? I'll pray on this and come up with other ideas. In the meantime, Drake, I suggest you make the time you do have with Noel important. Surprise her with things she likes, tell her how much you love and appreciate her. Pretend you're courting again and trying to win her heart. A lot of men think once they're married they can stop all that nonsense, but to your wife it's important. She wants to feel desired." Pastor Sheffield put his hand on Drake's shoulder. "If you two will make it to church on Sundays, I'm sure you'd find encouragement from others who care about you."

"Thanks, Pastor, I'll try. Having time for church is hard for me unless Albert is on duty Sunday mornings."

Pastor Sheffield hugged Drake. "Tomorrow is Thanksgiving. Spend the day with her and close up the sheriff's office. If there's an emergency they'll find you, otherwise, enjoy your time off. I'll be praying for both of you."

~

The aroma of bacon woke Drake from his dreams. A couple of brawls in the saloons kept him working late again. When he got home, he'd collapsed on the sofa.

It wasn't the best place to rest. His back hurt, so he tried stretching but nearly rolled off. Maybe he should sleep in the guest room, at least the bed would be comfortable. He followed the smell into the kitchen. Noel stood at the stove flipping pancakes.

"Who's coming for breakfast?" He grabbed a cup and poured himself coffee.

"No one. I wanted to make something special since it's Thanksgiving."

"That's nice of you, considering you'll be cooking most of the day." Drake sat at the table. "I didn't expect it. Do you need help?"

Noel brushed her hair back from her face. "No, it's mostly ready."

Her golden blonde hair hung loose, and Drake remembered how he loved to run his fingers through it even though it seemed like years ago. She wore a long nightgown with her bare toes peeking out from the hem. He wanted to wrap his arms around her and hold her close. He didn't, because if she resisted him, it might ruin the whole day.

Noel put two filled plates on the table. She'd made pancakes, bacon, and scrambled eggs.

"Did you ask Deputy Albert to dinner like I suggested? Noel sat in a chair and poured coffee into her cup.

Drake wiped his mouth. "I did, and he said he'd be here."

"Good, Violet will be here too. If you'll help me get the turkey cooking and wash dishes, I thought we might take a walk."

Drake almost tipped his chair over backwards as he'd leaned it back on two legs. If she'd slapped him, he couldn't have been more surprised. "Of course, I'd like that."

They spent the rest of the day cleaning, walking, and cooking. Drake didn't talk much, but they got into a rhythm of working together. He enjoyed having Albert and Violet over for dinner. There was lots to talk and laugh about. It made Thanksgiving even better. They both stayed until around ten. After helping Noel clean up the kitchen, they relaxed on the sofa in front of the fire with a cup of tea.

"It's been a great day Noel. I'm glad you wanted to invite the two of them over. They seemed to get along well."

"They did? I really enjoyed today. It was pretty much perfect." Noel glanced at him and smiled. The beautiful shape of her mouth made his thoughts turn to how inviting her lips were. He touched her face, and she didn't move away.

Drake moved closer to her and ran his fingers through her hair as his early morning wish came true. "Can I kiss you?" She closed her eyes and nodded yes as he gently touched her lips with his. It was like the first time they'd kissed. He stopped and looked at her. She wrapped her arms around his neck and they kissed again, this time with the passion of what months apart stirred in them. Drake stood and picked her up in his arms, she weighed nothing. He carried her up the stairs and sat her on their bed.

She lit a candle on the table next to the bed while he put wood on the embers in the hearth. The heat from the coals caught the logs on fire and it erupted into flames. Drake unbuttoned his shirt and threw it over the chair while Noel pulled the covers back.

He sat next to her and held her hand. Drake stared into the brown depths of her eyes. Love glistened brightly in them. He thought it had died, he should've taken the time to look. His lips brushed hers and she moved closer, pulling his mouth down to meet hers.

They didn't care about time as the feelings they'd stuffed for each other found new life. Drake had dreamed this moment would happen but dared not believe it.

Later, holding her in his arms and listening to her breathing softly in sleep, he realized how much he had to be thankful for.

Chapter Ten

Thanksgiving ended in the most wonderful way. Noel turned over and watched Drake sleep. She loved this man. He had so many good qualities; she wished spending time with her was one of them.

She touched his hair. His eyes popped open, and he looked surprised. Months had gone by since they'd slept in the same bed. Noel kissed him as he wrapped his arms around her and pulled her close.

Pounding on the front door interrupted what might have been. Drake kissed her on the cheek then got out of bed. He pulled on his pants and stuck his arms into his shirt to answer whoever was ruining their peaceful morning.

A few minutes later he came back to their room. "There's another ranch on fire. Sorry, Noel, but I have to leave. There are a few men headed out already."

Noel couldn't hide her disappointment. *Was it*

wrong to want the man you love with you? He put his socks and boots on as she sat up and pulled the blanket around her. The room cooled considerably.

"I don't want to leave you. I hope you know how much I wish I could stay."

Noel felt his longing for her in their kiss goodbye. She whispered, "I love you," as he walked out the door.

She had posted a sign on the bakeshop door saying it would be closed today. A day to do nothing, although, she wasn't good at being still. Coco jumped on the bed and curled up next to her. Well, maybe she'd do nothing for a little while. Her eyes shut, and she fell back to sleep.

Chapter Eleven

Drake fed and watered his horse. Steam rose from the heat of Gunner's sweaty coat as he brushed him. He barely felt his hands even with thick gloves on because the temperature had fallen so drastically. Drake couldn't wait to get inside the house and warm up. It was late, and he wanted to eat.

Only red-hot ashes and burned debris had greeted them when they made it to the ranch. When the foreman rode in soon after they arrived, Drake learned the family was visiting parents for Thanksgiving. The hired hands were driving cattle, so no one saw who set the fires. They'd have a hard time recovering from their losses, but they had each other, which is more than the McGregor's were left with.

It was arson. They found parts of the torches used to set the fires. Again, there wasn't a clear motive. These criminals must enjoy destroying lives for the sport of it or they were being hired to do this. Drake doubted they took much from inside the home. They weren't robbers, so he reasoned they were making money from the destruction.

How did these men stay hidden? Could they be townspeople? He'd hung a notice at the post office informing every one of the danger. He warned them to keep guards posted at their ranches and also suggested no one travel alone. Drake should follow his own advice.

A meeting was scheduled with the mayor today about hiring more deputies. Bozeman and the surrounding area had become a target and two lawmen weren't enough to cover it all. The mayor should realize how serious everything was getting.

Drake opened the back door and walked inside. Tucker and Maggie greeted him in the kitchen, licking his face as he crouched down to pet them. They didn't even bark when he unlocked the door. Great watchdogs, they'd lick you to death. Madam Susie had threatened to harm his wife, and he believed her capable of it. He needed to be home at night.

Drake stoked what was left of the fire and added more logs. He contemplated whether he should go upstairs and risk waking Noel or sleep down here. Either way, she might get upset. He probably didn't smell like honey after sifting through the ashes of the farmhouse and barn. A mixture of sweat, smoke, and horse wouldn't make a pleasant aroma. Sleeping on the sofa and sparing Noel the odor should be the best decision.

He went into the kitchen and grabbed a couple

of rolls from supper yesterday. He pulled them apart and put turkey and dressing inside. It tasted so good. He hadn't eaten since Thanksgiving dinner.

~

Drake had enjoyed the last two weeks since they'd found their way back to each other on Thanksgiving. Noel had spent time talking and sharing dreams with him again. He'd been home more at night.

Noel walked into the kitchen and kissed him. He wrapped his arms around her waist. "This is the best way to start the day." Drake hugged her. "Guess I should wash up. Are you going to the bakeshop today?"

"Yes, you should come by later and get some cinnamon rolls."

"I might. I need to go to the jail and make more signs to post around town informing every one about the new fire. If you wait until I get washed, I'll walk to the bakeshop with you."

"All right, but I need to leave soon, so don't take long."

Drake walked outside to the washbowl on the back porch.

Hoofbeats thundered toward their stable as Drake washed his face. He turned to see Kitchi and Hurit.

Kitchi was leading another horse. "We have gift for saving Hurit's life."

Drake walked over to them. "No need for a gift. You saved my life too, Kitchi."

"My father say take gift. If you not married, he give you Hurit as thank you. This is Wind Dancer, she excellent horse. Far better than Gunner." Kitchi snickered.

"Gunner's never failed me yet. I can't accept your father's horse." Drake walked over to the mare and patted her head.

Kitchi jumped off his horse. "My father have many horses. You have Wind Dancer."

"I'm not sure what to say. Tell your father many thanks." Drake took hold of Wind Dancer's halter.

Hurit dismounted and walked toward Drake. "I make good wife."

The back door opened, and Noel walked out. "Drake, what is taking so long?" She gasped when she saw Hurit standing by Drake.

"Kitchi's father gave me a horse for saving Hurit's life." Drake tied Wind Dancer to a post and walked over to his wife.

Hurit followed him. "I marry you at Crow camp."

Kitchi looked sheepishly at Noel. "She not understand white man ways, she want Drake have two wives. She defiled by white man, so no Crow brave marry her. Hurit's only hope is be Drake's wife."

Noel's face grew pale. "Drake! Why haven't you told me any of this?"

"I didn't know anything about Hurit wanting to be my wife. When I left, they weren't sure she would live. I had stopped at a creek to get water for Gunner and me and heard moaning. I found Hurit lying not far from where we drank water. She had been beaten, raped and left to die. I took her back to the Crow camp." Drake tried to touch Noel's shoulder, but she moved away.

Hurit grabbed Drake's arm. "Come back to camp. We have wedding."

Drake moved away. "I can't. I'm already married."

Hurit looked at Noel. "White woman too pale. I make better wife." Hurit wrapped both her arms around Drake's arm, this time not letting go.

"I can't Hurit, I love my wife, and I'm devoted to her. Besides, it's against the law. I'm glad you are getting better and in time one of the braves will marry you."

Drake realized this didn't bode well for him with Noel. Plus, Hurit had a death grip on his arm.

"I not want brave. I need lawman."

"Hurit!" Kitchi spoke Crow to her. She looked sad as she let go of Drake's arm and got back on her horse.

"Sorry, friend. I want her stay at camp but she followed. She wants make you happy for saving her life. She understand in time." Kitchi jumped back on his horse.

"Wind Dancer good horse, you should ride, instead of Gunner."

Drake laughed. "They're both good horses. Tell your father thank you. Hurit needs more time to heal, a husband can wait." Drake waved as they galloped away.

Noel had gone back into the house. He had explaining to do, and he hoped she'd understand.

~

The talk with Noel didn't go well. She was upset and crying because Drake never told her about

Hurit. When he explained how he'd held her on his horse to get her back to camp she got quiet. Noel accused him of keeping it from her because he had an interest in Kitchi's sister. She talked about how beautiful the Indian woman was and how she liked Drake. She didn't believe he hadn't expressed an interest in Hurit.

Drake sympathized with Hurit because of what those men did to her. No woman should have to endure such a horrendous crime. She'd have a hard time recovering not only physically but emotionally. She looked scared and wanted someone to protect her. He had to find those monsters and bring them to justice before they hurt anyone else.

Drake opened the door to the sheriff's office and walked inside. Albert sat behind the desk looking through papers.

"How is it going, Albert?"

"Quiet so far, but the day just started." Albert got up to pour himself more coffee. "Want a cup?"

"No thanks, I'm going to get breakfast at Mary's. Later today I'll be meeting with the mayor to see if we can hire more deputies. Neither of us should be riding alone. Remember when I told you about my run-in with Madam Suzie. I've been on edge since she made threats against Noel and I. The way she and Doc Bradford covered up the beating made me sick. The man is a snake."

"Yeah, it's been quite the last couple of weeks. We need help. I'll keep checking on the brothel and your home when you're away." Albert took another drink of his coffee. "I've been looking through the wanted posters but haven't seen any of these men around here."

Drake picked up the posters and looked through them. "I forgot to tell you and Noel, I found Kitchi's sister beaten and raped a few weeks ago. I took her back to their camp, and she survived. I bet it's the same men setting the fires who assaulted her. They must not be worried we'll catch them."

"Glad she pulled through. We can't handle everything with only the two of us."

"My worry is the corrupt business owners in our town who don't want more lawmen will keep pressure on the mayor to keep things the way they are. If the mayor keeps these owners happy, we won't get help. Which means the outlaws will continue killing whoever they want." Drake walked to the door. "I'll be gone for a few hours."

"We should quit if he doesn't allow you to hire more men. Let him and these business owners experience what it's like with no lawmen in Bozeman. I bet even the brothels and saloons would recognize how they need us to maintain some type of order." Albert followed Drake out the door. "I'm heading out to check on the town."

Drake walked over to Mary's restaurant. His thoughts were on Noel and he hoped she'd believe and forgive him. Their marriage, the last two weeks, had been better than it had been for a year. He had hope. She had to realize he loved her. Then again, maybe she didn't. He'd court his wife again like Pastor Sheffield suggested. He wanted to go by the bakeshop but decided he should give her time.

"Sheriff, come quick! There's a body in the

river."

Chapter Twelve

Noel cried all the way to the bakeshop. How could Drake not tell her something so important? This Crow woman had decided she'd be a better wife for him. He must've told her of their marriage problems. It hurt her to think about it.

Her conscious pricked her heart. Hadn't she allowed Mr. Steele in her life more than he should be? He'd made advances toward her and she didn't tell Drake or put a stop to it. Thank goodness Violet showed up when she did, or she may have let something happen she never intended to.

Noel wanted their marriage to get better. The last couple of weeks were the way it used to be. This morning those hopes crumbled. They'd let things go on being bad for too long. Now there were people trying to separate them.

Noel almost tripped over a basket by the door as she unlocked the bakeshop. She'd been so caught up in her thoughts she never noticed it. She picked it up and carried it inside. She lifted the blue fabric to reveal a lace fan. Noel fanned herself then put it back. Another mysterious gift. She doubted Drake left them, the only other person who came to mind was Mr. Steele. She didn't have time to bother with this now; she put the fan back in the basket and stuffed it in a cupboard in the kitchen.

A knock sounded at the door. Mary Sheffield stood outside. Noel forgot she'd asked her to come in this morning. "Good Morning, Mary."

"Morning, Mrs. West." Mary put on the pink flowered apron Violet made for her.

"If we're not busy, we'll get caught up on cleaning before the Christmas orders start." Noel handed Mary two different scone recipes. She helped her mother with cooking so Noel rarely needed to help her.

Noel was so focused on baking she didn't realize she should've opened five minutes ago. Customers waited outside the door.

"Good morning, Mrs. West."

Noel was taken aback. It was one of the Madams from the red-light district. She'd overheard people talk about her but Noel had never met her. Her brown hair was long and curly. She looked to be in her late thirty's, her beauty still apparent but wrinkles around her eyes and mouth made her look older.

"Let me introduce myself, everyone calls me Madam Suzie. So many of our clients have raved about your desserts, I decided I should try them." Everyone moved out of her way as she sauntered up to the counter.

Her blue velvet dress had lace on the end of each sleeve and down the train. Noel feared what might happen if she bent over. "I hope my baking is as good as you've been told."

Noel walked back around the counter to help Mary with the purchases.

Noel could tell Madam Suzie wished to talk with her. "Thank you, Mary, can you make another batch of scones? It's been busier than I anticipated it would be."

Madam Suzie stepped up to the counter. "I'll take twelve blueberry scones. A special treat for my girls this morning. I enjoyed seeing your husband the other evening. It's the first time he's been in my fine establishment. Hope everything is all right with the two of you.

He talked with one of my girls for a time before he left. I hope he's not trying to meet with her away from the brothel for a lesser amount. I won't allow that. Some wives don't mind their husbands paying my girls so they don't have to fulfill their wifely duties. Although, lawmen visiting my establishment doesn't happen often." She smiled, but it turned into a sneer.

"Here are your scones. I'm sure Drake had a good reason for being there and not the kind you are insinuating." Noel couldn't get this nasty woman out of her bakeshop fast enough. Why did she come out in public to tell her this? She must be worried Drake might entice this girl away or cause trouble for Madam Suzie. Noel hoped she was lying, otherwise, Drake would be someone she never really knew.

"Time will tell, won't it? In the meantime, you may want to keep an eye on your man." Madam Suzie paid for the scones and sashayed her hips as she walked out the door and down the sidewalk.

~

Noel locked the bakeshop door. What a crazy day. They'd baked more desserts because the customers never stopped. She had been impressed with Mary keeping up on all the baking.

Noel needed a few items at the mercantile to make dinner. She didn't look forward to talking with Drake, assuming he came home.

She crossed the street toward the mercantile and saw Drake walking down the alley behind the businesses. *Where is he going?* Noel decided to follow him. She stayed far enough away he shouldn't be able to see her. He walked around a small lake and into a stand of trees.

Noel wondered why he'd be going in there. As she snuck into the forest, she heard voices and silently made her way toward them. The sun was setting and only a few shafts of light shone through the gaps between trees. Noel saw the silhouette of a man and a woman standing close together. It had to be Drake. Her heart sank into the pit of her stomach.

She didn't understand what they were saying, so she crept forward. Sunlight glittered off rhinestones on the woman's dress and the low cut suggested she worked in the brothel. *Could Madam Suzie have been right?*

An intense conversation was occurring as the woman's voice grew louder. Then she recognized Drake's tone. It was him. Her world broke into a thousand pieces as he pulled the woman into his arms and she rested her head on his chest. *How dare he!*

Noel couldn't watch any more. She crept back out of the trees, and then ran around the lake. She walked up the stairs of a white pavilion to get control of her emotions before someone saw her. She sat on a bench, tears flowing down her cheeks, and took deep breaths.

"What's wrong, Mrs. West? Can I help you?" Mr. Steele walked up the steps into the pavilion.

Her tears stopped at the sight of him. *How did he always know where she was?*

"I received bad news from home." Noel lied.

"I'm very sorry, is there anything I can do." He sat next to her.

Noel wiped the remnants of tears from her cheeks. "No thank you. It's a personal issue. I'll have to work through it myself."

"I can leave if you'd rather be alone." Mr. Steele touched her shoulder.

"I'm all right and feeling a little better now." Noel glanced at him.

"If you don't have plans for dinner, we should eat at the motel, my treat. It might take your mind off things for a bit." Mr. Steele stood up.

"Oh, I'm sure my face is red and swollen. I should go home."

"You're a beautiful woman and a few tears doesn't change it." He held out his hand to help her up. "You don't want to be in that empty house alone."

Noel took his hand. Mr. Steele pulled her up

right into his chest. "You're gorgeous." He touched her chin and tilted her head up.

She tried to step back, but he held her tight.

"You have to know I'm attracted to you. I realize you're married, but from what I've seen, it doesn't seem like very happily. If I had a wife as enchanting as you, nothing would keep me away." His thumb brushed her lips and this time Noel jumped back.

"I'm sorry. I won't touch you, dinner and home. I promise I'll be the perfect gentleman."

"I should go home. I have too much on my mind and Drake will be there soon." Noel turned and went down the steps. "Thank you for the invitation."

"At least let me walk you home, it's getting dark."

"All right, thank you." They walked in silence to Noel's front door. There were no lights in the house. Drake must still be gone.

Mr. Steele looked at her as she unlocked her door. "I hope you get some rest. You have to be at your bakeshop early." Tucker and Maggie were barking inside.

"I'm going to try."

"I'm sorry Noel. I shouldn't have touched you. I forget myself around you. You needed a friend, not someone trying to seduce you. You take your marriage vows seriously."

"Thank you for saying that because your behavior was making me uncomfortable. I appreciate you walking me home. Good night, Mr. Steele."

"Good night, Mrs. West. I'll be the perfect gentleman."

Noel opened the door then closed and locked it behind her. That man is an enigma. He might be charming, but most of the time he'd been too forward. Hopefully, tonight Mr. Steele had gotten the message.

It didn't matter what Drake did or didn't do. Noel determined what was right for her. She decided not to mention seeing him with another woman. If he never brought it up, then she'd assume there was more than protecting the town going on when he was away.

Noel's thoughts turned to Mr. Steele. She hadn't been honest with Drake about the advances he made toward her. Although, she told Mr. Steele no. Drake never told the woman in the woods no. In fact, from what Noel saw, she looked quite at home in his arms.

Her insides boiled at the memory. How dare she lure her husband into the woods, although, he obviously went willingly. How many other women did she not know he spent time with? There were two she learned of today. Her stomach felt sick, so she left a note for Drake, asking him not to bother her, and headed upstairs to bed.

Chapter Thirteen

The door to the sheriff's office flung open. A blast of cold air accompanied Deputy Albert as he entered the room. "It's freezing out there. Drake, I thought you were going home last night." Albert added wood to the stove.

"I did, but I came in early, sleep isn't something that happens well on the sofa. Noel left a note saying she felt ill, so I didn't want to wake her." Drake filled the coffeepot.

"Any word on who the body in the river is?" Albert stomped the snow off his boots and it melted from the heat into small puddles.

"No one's claimed him, so we still have no idea. By the looks of the body, he'd been in there a few days. I'm guessing he floated into town from further upstream. Doesn't look like an outlaw, his clothes are too expensive. If he had papers on him someone took them. If no one claims him, he'll be buried in a day or so." Drake looked out the window, big snowflakes were falling fast.

Deputy Albert slung his coat over a chair. "It's sad when someone's life ends and no one knows who they are. There isn't anyone grieving his loss, no burial or headstone to remember him by."

Drake poured himself coffee. Steam rose from his cup and tickled his nose when he took a sip. "So many people come west hoping to get rich and only a few people ever meet them. They leave their families or their families are gone, so they're alone. They talk with the wrong men and end up in a life of wickedness."

"It is a hard life out here. I'll take some coffee, Drake. Anything exciting happen last night?"

"You might say so. I met with a prostitute named, Rose, from Madam Suzie's parlor. She, along with many of the girls there, are scared for their lives." Drake poured coffee into Albert's cup.

"How did you set the meeting up?"

"I told her if she had information to get a message to me on where and when we should meet. She slipped the note to a delivery boy, and he brought it to me yesterday afternoon. Madam Suzie has an abnormal revulsion for vomiting. So Rose made herself throw up, knowing she'd keep her away from the clients by having her stay in her room. She snuck out her window, risking a beating if she got caught.

I met her behind a lake in the woods last night. She told me our moral and trustworthy bank owner, Charles Steele, is a regular there and he repeatedly beats up the girls. Madam Suzie doesn't stop him because her loan for the building is through his bank. Rose believes he threatens foreclosure if she stands up to him.

Madam Suzie despises him and his threats. She doesn't appreciate him hitting her girls because it keeps them from working and making her money. Steele must find pleasure in abusing them because it happens almost every time he visits. He's never asked for Rose but she's afraid he will. It was her friend Della he beat up the night I went in there. She stayed in bed for five days because of those injuries he gave her."

Deputy Albert whistled. "Wow, I would never have guessed he'd beat up women, much less visit a brothel. I guess you can never tell by appearances or what type of work someone does. My stepfather used to hit my mother. Men who strike women are vermin. I'd love to give him a taste of his own medicine, handcuff him and throw him in jail."

"It would be a pleasure to lock him up. Because of his prominence in town, he thinks he's above the law. I've seen him being too friendly with my wife at the bakeshop. He better watch himself."

"Well, I'm going home to feed and water the horses. Did I tell you Kitchi brought me a horse as a gift from his father? He wanted to thank me for saving Hurit. I told him Gunner is a good horse, and I didn't need another. Kitchi insisted, so I kept her. She's quite the beauty, her name is Wind Dancer."

"I'm sure you're looking forward to riding her to see if she lives up to her name."

Drake put his coat on. "I am! Being a Crow horse, she'll be well trained. I hope Gunner won't think I'm neglecting him. Gunner is a great horse, but as much riding as I do, it would be good to give him some rest days. I'll be back later."

Drake walked out the door into the swirling snow. The buildings across the street were silhouettes through the whiteout. Riding Wind Dancer would have to wait for another day. This storm might turn into a full-fledged blizzard. He needed to split wood, their pile was getting low.

~

Drake chopped wood until his back protested to the point he had to stop. Six inches of snow had accumulated, and it wasn't letting up. Noel should be home soon.

He split the last two pieces and dusted himself off. He carried an armload of wood to their back porch and stacked it with the rest he'd done. The crunch of footsteps in the snow caused him to turn around.

"Sheriff West."

Drake recognized Rose's voice. She stood a few feet away shivering from the cold. She wore a full-length coat with a hood which covered most of her face.

"I can't go back there again. You have to help me. They'll kill me next time. Someone found out I talked to you and Mr. Steele paid me a visit last night. The man is an animal." Rose pushed her hood back to reveal her bruised and cut face. One eye was only a slit because of the swelling. Her lips cut and swollen. "The rest of me don't look no better."

"I'm so sorry Rose. I should've realized someone would trail us. Would you testify against Steele so we can put him in jail?"

"No. I'd be signing my death certificate. His men would find me. If you won't help me, I'll leave on the next train out-of-town tomorrow."

Drake had to get her somewhere safe. "Let's take you to the jail. I'll put you in the back cell where no one can see you. Either I or Deputy Albert will be there to make sure you're safe until we figure out the next step. We need to go now. Cover your face with the hood."

"Thank you, but I want to get out of town right away." Rose pulled her hood down over her face.

"It'll only be temporary. I'll get you out-of-town as soon as it's possible. They'll be looking for you. When they decide you're gone for good is when we'll put you on a train." The snow fell harder, so he hoped no one recognized her. He'd be spending his night at the jail since he couldn't leave her alone. Someone might have followed her to his house.

They walked through the back gate and down the side streets. At the sheriff's office, he explained the situation to Deputy Albert. Albert went to get food for them from Mary's Restaurant and then they'd decide on a plan.

Drake led Rose to the back jail cell in case someone walked in. He handed her clean blankets and a pillow. "It's not the nicest accommodations but you'll be safe."

"Safe is better than the softest pillow or warmest quilt." Rose sat on the cot.

"I'll make coffee and when Albert gets back, we'll bring your food to you. It won't be easy being here, but you have to stay quiet and out of sight."

Drake walked up front. He'd need to find her a change of clothes. Some books to read might help her pass the time. She'd have to relieve herself in a bucket, as they wouldn't risk her going outside. It was the price of keeping her safe.

He wanted to arrest Steele but without her testimony, he had no evidence. Even if she did testify, he'd need more than a prostitute's word against him to get a conviction. Steele had to be stopped before he killed someone.

Noel would never understand any of this and he couldn't blame her. He left before she came home. Drake felt, as Sheriff, it was his responsibility to make sure nothing happened to Rose. Although, what kind of husband abandons his wife, especially when Madam Suzie has threatened her? There had to be a better solution. It had to be easy, though, as he only had Albert to help. The mayor hadn't gotten back to him about hiring more deputies. Typical politician. The situations in his life weren't getting better, only worse. How much longer must he wait before he got some help?

Chapter Fourteen

Noel closed the front door, another long day at the bakeshop. Maggie and Tucker ran to greet her. She hung up her snow-covered coat, gloves, and hat while each dog bounced in circles around her. She wondered if Drake had come home; she noticed the quilt on the sofa had been moved when she came downstairs this morning.

She walked through the house and went out to the back porch. She glanced around the yard but didn't see him. She peered toward the other side of their property and noticed two people leaving through a gate. It was Drake and a woman. She couldn't make out any features as the hood covered most of her face and the snow falling made it hard to identify who it might be.

She considered yelling but he wouldn't hear her. *What is going on? Did she really know Drake?* Even though things were difficult between them, she never imagined he'd turn to another woman.

Someone knocked at her front door. She didn't want to answer it. The last thing she needed was company. The knocking increased. Noel made herself open the door. It was Violet.

"What took you so long? It's freezing out here." Violet walked in and put her coat and boots by the door. "It's cold in here too."

"I haven't been home long. Let me check the fireplace." There aren't any hot coals. "I'll bring in some wood and get a fire going. Would you mind filling the stove in the kitchen so we can have tea?"

"Sure."

The pile of wood on the back porch had increased significantly, at least he'd done something to help. She grabbed an armload and walked inside.

"There were coals in the stove, so I added some wood and it's taking off." Violet followed Noel into the sitting room.

Noel got the wood lit and used the bellows to get it blazing. "It's going great now. Let me heat some water."

"Where's Drake? I noticed him splitting wood earlier."

"I'm not sure. I haven't seen much of him the last couple of days." Noel grabbed cups and tea and sat across from Violet at the kitchen table.

"Really, I hoped you two were doing better. On Thanksgiving Day, Drake and you laughed and smiled, it felt like old times."

"It did get better for a couple of weeks but it's falling apart now. He might be involved with two women. Kitchi's sister and one of Madam Suzie's girls." Noel tried to stop a sob from escaping.

"Madam Suzie even came by the bakeshop to tell me Drake was secretly meeting her girls."

"Oh honey, there has to be a logical explanation. Have you asked him about it?" Violet put her hand on top of Noel's.

"He insisted there was nothing between him and Kitchi's sister, Hurit. Yet, he never told me about finding her in the forest beaten and raped. He held her in his arms for miles on horseback as he took her back to the Crow camp. She came here with, Kitchi, who brought a horse as a thank you from her father to Drake. Hurit said she wanted to marry Drake and be a good wife to him.

Last night, I noticed him walking down an alley on my way to the mercantile so I followed him. He met a lady behind the lake in the trees. He held her in his arms as she cried. When I got home tonight, I caught him leaving with a woman out the back gate. I couldn't see her face." Noel broke down into heart-wrenching sobs. Violet put her arm around her.

"I'm sure he didn't have any other way to get Kitchi's sister back to camp or he would have. This woman might be in trouble and asked him for help. Why would Drake be interested in a prostitute when he has you?" Violet gave her a hug. "There must be a good explanation for all of this."

"I wish I believed all you said. If there is a reason why does he not tell me? I'm alone in this house most nights. Should another woman's troubles come before mine? Should he be holding another woman in his arms, comforting her, when I need him to hold me? If he loved me, would this be how he acted? He's so busy saving the world, he has no time to save me." Noel regained her composure and took a sip of tea. "I'm sorry. I never even asked why you came over. I haven't been a good friend lately. I'm trying to be strong, but it hurts."

Violet hugged Noel again. "It's all right. I came over to visit you. You are strong. When my parents died and left me alone in Montana, I wondered how I would live with all the pain. I pleaded to God to take me to heaven with them. He refused, but He sent me a friend who convinced me I'd get through it. No matter what is happening, Noel, you'll find a way. Don't give up on Drake yet."

"My heart is crushed. I doubt I will ever forgive him if any of this is true. I love him, but if I'm going to be alone, then I might as well live alone. Can we change the subject? Will you eat dinner with me?" Noel appreciated having Violet as a friend. She had to talk to someone about everything going on in her life, and she trusted her.

"Of course. Let's make something together."

~

Alma Sheffield came into the bakeshop after Noel arrived to tell her Mary wouldn't be in. She had an upset stomach. Alma said Emma, her thirteen-year-old offered to come in and help, but Noel didn't want to hear about Drake's best attributes. Emma believed him to be the best at everything, because he'd saved her from the flood, so Noel passed on the help.

Noel had used her last egg and still needed to make pastries. She hoped Mildred or Ben came soon. As quick as she thought it, someone knocked on the door.

Noel opened it. "Hello, Mildred, I'm glad you're here."

"Sorry, I'm late dear. Our wagon wheel came loose and Ben spent a good amount of time getting it tightened back up. I'm thankful he carries the tools needed to work on things." Mildred carried the crates to the kitchen.

"I'm glad he fixed it and am doubly glad you're here as I used my last egg. Mary is sick today, so I'm on my own. I won't be doing any more baking after this, if we run out I'll close early." Noel cracked an egg into her flour mixture.

"You might have to hire another helper. I'll have to buy more chickens and cows to keep up with you." Mildred laughed.

"I never dreamed business would increase so fast. I'm thankful, but it's a bit overwhelming too. I should ask, Emma, Mary's sister. Her mother suggested she help today, and I turned her down. Guess I should've considered it more seriously." Noel rolled out the dough and then cut it into large circles. She placed apples, sugar, and spices in the center of each one, folded it over and sealed the edges.

"You're so fast. I'd still be making the dough." Mildred leaned against the wall. "How are you and Drake?"

Noel told her everything she'd said to Violet the night before, only without the tears. Mildred agreed there had to be more to the story. After she left, Noel tried to give Drake the benefit of the doubt.

Although, skepticism kept popping up. The picture of Drake embracing a woman had been seared into her mind.

The day turned out to be slow. She caught up the cleaning and worked off some frustration. She just finished mopping the kitchen when the bell jingled. Mr. Steele. She walked to the counter.

"How are you, Noel? I've been craving a chocolate cupcake and took a chance you might still have one this late in the day."

"I have a couple left. You're in luck." Noel got them from the kitchen. "At least, I'm not a bucket of tears today."

"I hope the reason for those tears has gotten better." Mr. Steele tried to pay her for both cupcakes.

"The second one is free. In case you need more chocolate than you anticipated." Noel put them in a small box.

"Thank you. I won't have a problem eating them both. Your desserts are the best I've ever tasted. My cook is no match for you."

"Thank you. Rumors are your cook makes delicious meals." Noel smiled. She liked this version of Mr. Steele.

"She does indeed. I have yet to go hungry. Well, good night, I hope you have an enjoyable evening and I'm glad you're better." He picked up the box and left.

Noel put on her coat and locked up. Snow continued falling, she longed for sunshine again. She'd taken a few steps when someone grabbed her from behind. She screamed before a hand clasped over her mouth. The person pulled her into an alley by the bakeshop. She kicked and hit trying to get loose.

"Stop fighting or I'll cut your throat." A deep voice whispered in her ear. He shoved her face into a wall. "Your husband is a little too nosey. You might persuade him to back off if he wants his wife alive. I'm sure a pretty thing like you would know how to change a man's mind."

Bile rose in Noel's throat and dizziness made her grasp for the wall. He might be disgusted and leave if she threw up on him. "I don't know what my husband does."

"He sticks his nose where it shouldn't be. He ought to be home with his loving wife instead of secretly meeting prostitutes. The boss doesn't like it." The man shoved her into the wall with his body. The bricks dug into her face. She caught a glimpse of a knife blade in his hand. The tip pierced her neck. She cried out, and he pressed it in more. "A reminder of our conversation."

Terror swept Noel. Her knees gave way. All of a sudden, the man's weight against her was yanked away. She crumpled to the ground. Noel turned in time to see Mr. Steele punching the man in the face. He fell, rolled to the side, jumped up, and ran off.

"I'd go after him, but my time would be better spent making sure you're all right." Mr. Steele reached for Noel's hand.

Tears streamed down her cheeks and her body shook from head to toe. She wrapped her arms around herself. Mr. Steele picked her up, as she cried uncontrollably and hid her face in his jacket.

He should let her walk, she was a married woman, but she doubted her ability to stand at the moment. She felt blood running down her neck and worried how deep the monster had cut her. Mr. Steele's butler opened the front door, and he carried her to a sofa. He spread a blanket over her from a chair nearby. Blood stained his vest. He grabbed a handkerchief from his pocket and put it over her wound.

"Sir, would you like me to get help?" The butler asked.

"Get Doc Bradford and tell him it's an emergency and have one of the maids bring me a towel."

"Yes sir, right away."

"Noel, what can I do?" Mr. Steele held the cloth on her neck.

Her teeth chattering kept her from answering. The maid brought a towel and a cup of water. "Would you like a drink?" Noel shook her head no. They sat in silence while he kept pressure on the cut.

Someone knocked at the front door and a man followed the butler in. "What's the problem, Charles?"

"This is Sheriff West's wife. A man assaulted her in the alleyway by her bakeshop. I was only a short distance away when I heard her scream, so I ran to her aide. She has a deep cut on her neck and other cuts and bruises on her face, so I wanted you to take a look at them."

"Certainly. It's a good thing you were there, Charles. Is there a room we can move her to?"

"Yes, we'll take her to a guest room on this floor." He picked Noel up and carried her down a hall. He laid her on the bed. "I'll be outside if you need me, Doc."

The doctor tried asking Noel questions, but she only managed a couple of nods. He cleaned her cuts and gave her something to help her relax. He told her he'd have to do a few stitches on her neck. The sedative worked quickly, and she wondered if the stitches would hurt. Her eyelids grew heavy, and she succumbed to sleep.

Chapter Fifteen

Drake rode into the stable. He hoped Noel would be awake. He'd spent last night at the jail with Rose and Albert.

This morning they decided to take Rose to the Crow camp and ask the missionaries if they'd let her stay with them. The snow fell heavily all day, so it took twice as long as normal. When they arrived at the Crow camp Drake explained to the missionaries what Rose had been through. They told her she could live in a teepee next to them until she could return to town.

The missionaries were a couple with a small child. They had been teaching the tribe how to speak English and how much Jesus loved them. Drake admired their courage. It wouldn't be easy to go to a people completely different from themselves and teach them.

Rose looked frightened the whole day. Drake wondered if she'd stay when he left. He didn't blame her, it wouldn't be easy. Once the missionaries committed to her living next to them Rose relaxed and expressed her gratitude. Kitchi promised to watch over her and the tribe agreed for her to live there.

Hurit had spent considerable time trying to convince Drake of the reasons he should take her for a wife. Again, Kitchi had to speak with her. She had determination, he had to give her that. Before Hurit left, she gave Kitchi a look that would scare a lesser man.

It was early evening. Drake brushed Gunner and watered the three horses. He hoped to repair the damage of the last couple of days with Noel, so they could continue making their marriage better. He tried to prepare himself in case she didn't accept his story. She'd been mad enough over Hurit and now he'd be bringing Rose into the conversation.

Noel should be home, but there weren't any lights flickering in the house. He opened the back door and went in. Tucker and Maggie greeted him with tail wags. It was freezing inside. He checked the stove in the kitchen and the fireplace in the sitting room; the ashes were cold to the touch. *Did Noel come home after work?* It didn't look like it. He ran up the stairs to check the bedrooms, but she wasn't there.

Tucker and Maggie jumped on his legs, then ran downstairs to their dog bowl. Noel fed them when she got home from the bakeshop every night. He followed them and put food and water in their bowls. *Did she go to Violet's before coming here?*

Thoughts of something happening to Noel crept

into his mind while knots formed in his stomach. He ran to Violet's house and pounded on the door.

"Goodness Drake, what's wrong?" Violet stepped out onto the porch.

"Have you seen Noel tonight?" He pushed his hair back out of his eyes. He'd left his hat in the house.

"I haven't. I had dinner with her last night but I've been busy sewing and hadn't even bothered to check if she was home. Did she stay late at the bakeshop?"

"I doubt it, but I'm going to make sure." Drake ran down the steps.

Violet hollered. "Tell me when you find her."

Drake ran all the way to the shop. It was dark inside, and the door was locked. He didn't have a key. He had never asked Noel if there was an extra one. Drake ran to the sheriff's office to check if she'd stopped there.

Drake burst through the door of the jail so fast it made Albert jump in his chair. Drake scanned the room but didn't see her. "Albert, have you seen Noel?"

"I came here after we got back, and she hasn't been by."

"She isn't at the house, or Violet's, or the bakeshop and now she's not here." Drake plopped into a chair. "Where could she be?"

"I'm sorry Drake. Would she have gone to the hotel or Mary's to eat?" Albert put more wood in the stove.

"I doubt it but I'll check." Drake ran across the street and went into both businesses. No one had seen her.

Drake walked back to the jail. "No one has seen her tonight."

"She might be out visiting Mildred."

"After her last experience going out there, I don't think she would go alone. I can't go out there this late." Drake paced the floor. "What if she's lying in the snow somewhere?"

"Let's go to the shop and make sure she's not in there. We'll check along the streets between the bakeshop and your house." Albert grabbed his coat.

"I don't have a key, we'll have to break in. Wait, Mary Sheffield might have an extra key. She's been helping Noel the last few weeks at the bakeshop." Drake went out the door.

They walked to the Sheffield's at a swift pace. No one talked. Pastor Sheffield answered the door. "Good evening Drake. How are you, Albert? Come on in, is everything all right?"

"Noel is missing, is she here?"

"No, I'm afraid she's not."

"Did Mary work with her today? Does she have a key to the bakeshop?" Drake looked around. Emma sat in a chair reading a book.

"Mary's been sick, so she didn't go to the bakeshop today. But, if you give me a minute, I'll ask her about the key." Pastor Sheffield walked out of the room.

Emma looked at Drake. "I hope you find her soon. I'll be praying."

"Thank you, Emma." Drake felt his eyes get watery.

Pastor Sheffield returned and handed a key to

Drake. "She did have one. Would you like me to help you search?"

"Yes, I'd appreciate your help." Drake tucked the key into his pants pocket.

"Let me tell, Alma, I'll be leaving for a while."

All three men searched the bakeshop. She wasn't there, and nothing seemed out of place.

Drake looked at Albert and Pastor Sheffield. "I should've never left her alone after Madam Suzie threatened her."

"Why would Madam Suzie threaten Noel?" Pastor Sheffield asked.

Drake told the pastor everything that had happened the last few weeks.

"Wow, I had no idea any of this was going on in our town. I assumed, Mr. Steele was a gentleman and a man of honor. This certainly changes everything I've believed about him. Of course, the brothels are awful places where sin runs rampant and nothing is off limits. I'm also surprised to hear of Doc Bradford's part in all of this. He's never been, my favorite physician. Doctor Brown has a much better bedside manner, but I didn't think badly of Doc Bradford.

The body in the river hasn't been identified. The fires and murders on the ranches, and the assault on the Crow woman. Is any of this connected, or has our valley turned into a haven of lawlessness and gangs? You need more deputies, and you need them now." Pastor Sheffield said in his best Sunday sermon voice.

"It's time for me to check for her in the not-so-safe places. Why don't you and Albert split up and search the side streets on your way back to my house, and I'll meet you there later."

Drake was fuming as he ran to Madam Suzie's. When he got there, a couple of girls stood outside the front door half dressed, trying to lure men in.

One of the girls winked at him and dropped the strap down off her shoulder. "Why sheriff, are you making a pleasure call? We never thought you'd visit us. We heard you were smitten with your pretty wife."

"No, I'm not." Drake yelled. "I need to speak with Madam Suzie now." He flung the door open and headed toward the stairs. "Which room is hers?"

"She won't like you barging in, Sheriff." A voice yelled.

"I don't care what she likes." Drake started busting doors open. Girls screamed, and the clients were a bit surprised as he made his way from room to room. At the end of the hall, he flung the door wide to the room he'd been searching for. Madam Suzie sat behind a desk in a red and black lace gown.

"Why, Sheriff West, if you wanted me all you had to do was ask. Not interrupt my whole business." She swayed her hips as she walked toward him.

"I'm in no mood for your deceit. Where's my wife?"

"Oh dear, the poor sheriff has misplaced his wife." Madam Suzie walked over to him and wrapped one arm around his neck, she trailed her fingers down his face with her other hand. "Did you not pay attention to what I warned you about? What a shame it would be if you didn't locate her. Although, you might decide my girls are more appealing. Your wife seems a bit cold." She ran her finger along his lips.

Drake shoved her away. "You disgust me and if you've hurt her in any way, you and whoever else is responsible will hang."

"You'll never convict me of anything. I have so many little secrets I can tell, no one will let you touch me. I had nothing to do with your wife's disappearance. I tried to warn you to mind your own business, but you didn't listen. There are forces at play all around us and they're far more powerful than I'll ever be. I'm a small town brothel owner, providing a service for the men and trying to keep my girls safe. You're looking in the wrong place, Sheriff. Now, please leave!" Madam Suzie turned her back on him.

Drake gripped her upper arms and turned her around. "If you hear anything at all, tell me! If I discover you didn't, I'll be your worst enemy. I will make it my goal to close this place and ruin your reputation if I can't keep you behind bars."

Drake let go and stomped from the room yelling. "If anyone knows where my wife is, they better come forward with the information." He went down the stairs and slammed the front door so hard the whole building shook.

Drake walked to his house. Albert and Pastor Sheffield should be there by now. He opened the back door, they were sitting at the kitchen table talking.

"Drake, what did you find out? We searched along the side streets all the way from the bakeshop to here and we didn't discover her or notice anything unusual. We even looked around your property. We got your house warmed up and made some coffee."

"Madam Suzie claims she isn't involved. Pretty much what I expected. I told her if anything happens to Noel and she's responsible or knows who is, I'll watch her hang. If not, she'll be put behind bars, and her livelihood ruined."

"I'm sorry." Pastor Sheffield stood up. "Drake, can I pray for you and Noel? You've both been through so much. I don't understand how you're even standing."

"Of course."

They bowed their heads as Pastor Sheffield prayed for Noel's safe return. He stood and got his coat off the back of the chair. "There's not much else to do tonight. I say we try to get a couple of hours of sleep, then meet up at daybreak. We'll round up more men to help search. I'll continue to pray throughout the night."

Albert put his coat on. "I'll stay at the jail in case someone comes in with any information. If you need me, come get me. See you in the morning."

"I appreciate you both. I'm going to ride out to Mildred's first thing, then I'll meet you both at the jail." Drake followed them to the door and locked it behind them as they left.

If he'd only stayed in town today, Noel might be here with him. Drake left before she even made it home last night and hadn't checked on her before they rode out to the Crow camp. He got so wrapped up in keeping Rose safe, he put his wife in danger. He had been warned but didn't take it seriously.

~

Drake rode to Mildred's yellow farmhouse as the sun peeked over the mountains. Ben walked toward the barn with a dog following behind. Drake jumped off Gunner. "Does Noel happen to be out here? She never came home last night."

"No, Sheriff, I haven't seen her since I took mother there yesterday to drop off eggs, butter, and milk. Do you need help searching? I can head into town as soon as I get the cows milked." Ben patted Drake on the back.

"If you can help search, I'd appreciate it. We checked with everyone she knows, searched the bakeshop and side streets. No one saw her. You were my last hope of finding her with someone safe." Drake mounted Gunner.

"I'm sorry, Sheriff, I wish your wife was here. I'll tell mother and she'll pray. I know mother will be upset. As soon as I finish up here, I'll meet you in town."

Drake took off on Gunner. As he neared the sheriff's office, twenty men stood outside. His emotions got the better of him and a tear fell from his eye. *God, if it's not too late, please help me find my wife.*

Chapter Sixteen

Noel opened her eyes as panic seized her. Where was she? "Someone help me." She screamed.

The door opened, and Mr. Steele walked in. "What's wrong, Mrs. West? Do you need the doctor again? Here, take a sip of water." He took a cup from the table and helped hold her head as she swallowed.

"Why am I here with you?" She laid back down. Noel could hardly move her body it had no energy.

"Don't you remember? A man grabbed you after you'd locked up the bakeshop and pulled you into an alley. He shoved you against a building and you were hurt. I'd just left you a minute before when I heard your screams. I ran back to help you and carried you to my home. Doc Bradford has been attending to your injuries." He patted her hand.

"Has someone told my husband?" Noel remembered a man grabbing and pulling her into the alley and cutting her neck but she didn't remember much after.

Mr. Steele sat in a chair beside the bed. "Of course, we told his deputy where you are. He said Sheriff West left yesterday morning and hadn't returned. I assured the deputy you were being taken care of and Sheriff West should come for you as soon as he gets back to town."

"Please take me home. I'm sure my neighbor Violet will look after me." Noel tried to sit up but barely lifted her head and the room spun. "Why am I so weak?"

"Doc Bradford says you sustained a concussion when your head was slammed against the wall. You lost blood from your neck being cut. It may take a few days for you to regain your strength. Your attacker roughed you up. I think it best not to move you until your husband is home to see to your needs. I have servants here to help." Mr. Steele took hold of her hand. "I'm not that bad, Mrs. West, and I promise to take good care of you."

Drowsiness tried to pull her under. She tried to move her hand, but it weighed too much.

Mr. Steele bent over and kissed her on the cheek. "You are a beautiful woman, Noel. We'll have time to get to know each other better."

Alarms ran through every nerve of Noel's body but all she could do was succumb to the sleep which overtook her.

Chapter Seventeen

The men split up into groups of three or four and spent over ten hours searching for Noel. They searched every back street and alleyway, and through farmlands outside of Bozeman with no luck. Word spread through town Noel was missing, yet no one came forward to say they saw her. Many had bought desserts from her at the bakeshop the day she vanished.

Drake put Gunner in his stall for the night and opened the back door. The house felt so cold. He lit a fire in the kitchen stove.

The adrenaline from the search had worn off, and he felt empty. He wondered before how life would be without Noel if they didn't heal their marriage. His imaginings never came close to how it actually felt. How could he carry on doing normal things apart from his wife? *Where are you, Noel?*

A draft of cold air wrapped around him. Where were the dogs? They didn't run to greet him. Had they gotten out? He locked the front door this morning. He made his way through the sitting room to the fireplace in the dark, he almost tripped over something. He bent to pick it up. A sudden pain to the back of his head caused everything to go black.

~

The buzzing in his ears faded as he faintly heard someone calling his name.

"Drake, wake up!" It came clearer now. Someone shook his shoulders as he opened his eyes. His head hurt as if it was in a vise. The room spun as he tried to sit up.

"Don't get up. Your head has been bleeding badly and you have a nasty lump on the back of it."

Drake focused on who was talking. Violet and Albert were beside him.

Albert knelt closer to Drake. "Did you notice who hit you?"

"No, it was dark, and I almost tripped as I bent over to pick up something on the floor. That's the last thing I remember. Can I get some water?" Drake's words came out in whispers because of his dry throat.

"Of course." Violet got up and went to the kitchen.

"You almost tripped on this. Deputy Albert held up a piece of firewood. Someone waited in the sitting room for you. They must've caused another piece to roll off the pile when they got the one they hit you with. There was a note beside you. Do you want me to read it or do you think you can?"

"I can read it."

Albert handed the note to Drake.

Sheriff West,

By now you've realized your wife is nowhere to be found. You should've kept her safe. If you want to see her again, resign as sheriff and move back to where you came from. We'll reunite her with you in Denver. If you do not follow these instructions, you'll never be with her again.

Violet returned with a cup of water. "Let's help you sit up."

Albert put his arm under his back and lifted him to a sitting position. The room spun as Drake took a sip of water. Violet grabbed a pillow and Albert laid him down.

"The doctor should be here any minute." Violet patted Drake's hand. "Most of the bleeding stopped but you have a large gash on the back of your head."

"I guess we don't have to search anymore. Obviously, someone kidnapped Noel and won't release her until I go back to Denver. It's just a ploy to get me out of town because I'm catching on to them.

I wonder if Madam Suzie is involved in kidnapping Noel or she may be part of a larger group who is. They might be responsible for the murders and ranch fires. I don't understand the connection yet but it's too coincidental. They must think the next sheriff will follow their bidding." Drake rolled on to his side. "I'm going to be sick."

Violet ran and brought a bowl to him just in

time. Every involuntary movement sent sharp pains through his head.

Doctor Brown arrived and examined Drake's head. He had suffered a concussion which caused the dizziness and nausea. The doctor gave Drake a few shots of whiskey and numbed the wound to help with the pain before he sewed it up.

They lifted Drake off the floor and onto the sofa. Violet said she'd spend the rest of the day taking care of him. Albert volunteered to stay the night and talk to Pastor Sheffield about getting other people to help out.

"Oh, Maggie and Tucker were sitting on my front porch this morning. When I noticed them I knew something happened. I'll keep them over there until you're up to having them back." Violet laid the quilt over him.

Drake realized how Noel made this house a home. His family lived in Denver and there weren't many he would call a friend. He wondered how to get word to, Kitchi. He needed help. A wire should be sent to the Governor of Montana to ask for more lawmen.

Doctor Brown gave him a sedative, and his eyes kept shutting. They could use a break, a clue, someone coming forward.

"Albert, send a wire to the Governor asking for help." Drake drifted off.

Chapter Eighteen

The sound of a door shutting caused Noel to open her eyes. Despair filled her heart as no one waited in the room for her to wake up. *Where is Drake?* Did he leave town with the prostitute from Madam Suzie's? She hoped he'd be here to take her home when she woke up and they'd talk through everything that happened. *Did Albert tell him where I am? Why hasn't anyone checked on me?* It didn't make sense. She'd been taken to a different world.

Her arms were weak but getting stronger. She couldn't sleep anymore because she needed to return to running her bakeshop. After a few attempts, she managed to sit up and keep herself upright. *Should I try to stand? I don't want to fall.*

The door opened, and Mr. Steele walked in. "You're awake, how perfect. I brought some water for you to freshen up, if you need help I'll summon a maid. I'm going to carry you out to my garden for some fresh air. You'll enjoy it. There's a clean dress for you to put on. The maids will tell me when you're ready."

"I'll need help," Noel stammered.

"Of course."

The maid helped Noel freshen up and get the dress on. By the time they'd finished, she'd exhausted all her energy.

Mr. Steele walked back in and picked her up as if she weighed hardly anything. He carried her to a garden behind the house. Trees and bushes enclosed the area. Prying eyes couldn't see what happened inside this secret hide-a-way. It was lovely even though nothing was growing this time of year. Quiet and peaceful. A maid brought a quilt out for her as Mr. Steele set her on a bench. He put the blanket around Noel and sat next to her.

"How are you feeling?"

"Weak and tired."

"You've been through a lot. Doc Bradford says it won't be long and you'll be well. I'm sorry, but no one has come by. I've been told your husband hasn't returned, he never told anyone where he was going. I hate to say this, but there are rumors he left with one of Madam Suzie's prostitutes."

Noel looked up at him, tears forming in her eyes. "Why?"

"I don't understand it either. You are a beautiful woman, Noel, why would he leave you?" He kissed Noel on the forehead while he wiped her tears away with his thumb.

Mr. Steele cared about her. Why had she been uncomfortable around him before? Drake left her and took another woman with him. He hadn't been there to protect her. They sat in silence for a few minutes.

"Are you cold?"

"A little."

Mr. Steele drew her into his side. "I would never leave you if you were my wife, Noel."

The warmth from him relaxed her, and soon her eyelids closed.

~

It had to be midafternoon when Noel woke. The sun was high in the window of her room. Had she slept through the rest of yesterday, last night, until now? Why was she sleeping so much?

Mr. Steele walked in. "I have fruit and water for you and have planned a special dinner for us. The maids will be in shortly to help you bathe and dress. I hope it helps you get better.

Noel was famished, she didn't remember the last time she'd eaten. She devoured the entire plate of fruit, but her stomach still rumbled. A little energy returned as the maids brought in a bathtub and filled it with warm water. She wanted to be clean again. She hadn't bathed since the man had hurt her.

"Mr. Steele said to be careful of your neck where the stitches are." One of the maids helped steady her into the bath. "Ring this bell when you are ready to get out."

Noel sunk into the warm depths as she completely relaxed for the first time in days. She had to focus on getting better. She'd put the bakeshop up for sale and go back to Denver, away from this town and its reminders of Drake. She soaked until the water cooled, then rang the bell. The maids helped her dress.

The gown was beautiful in shades of red and black. The neckline lower than Noel normally wore but not too distasteful. One of the maids put a necklace around her with a red glass heart. She now had her answer to who left her the gifts. Her heart ached for all she'd lost with Drake. They misted her with a floral fragrance and led Noel to the formal dining room.

Candles were lit around the room. The dark cherry wood furniture was intricately carved. A crystal chandelier hung from the middle of the ceiling. Mr. Steele put her hand on the inside of his elbow and seated her next to him.

"Your house is stunning."

"No, my dear, you're stunning. I'm glad you like it. I wanted it to be the home I would raise my family in."

"The necklace is beautiful, thank you. I assume you're the mysterious gift giver?

"I am." Mr. Steele lifted the glass heart from her neck. "I wanted to show you how special you are. I know your husband didn't."

Noel gasped. *Did everyone know?* "The duties of sheriff kept him busy. Do you have family close by?"

"No, my parents passed away before I came to Montana. With my inheritance, I decided to open a bank. My father taught me the banking business at a young age. I'd never found the right woman until I saw you."

"I'm married."

"To a man who doesn't deserve you?"

The maids served them tomato soup. The soup tasted like the kind Mrs. Maples had made for them in Denver. "I miss my parents. They're alive, but they live in Colorado." Noel dabbed her lips with her napkin.

The main course was served, and they talked of their families and living in Montana through the rest of dinner. A big piece of chocolate cake with vanilla icing made the perfect end to the meal. Noel was stuffed.

"Your cook is a wonderful baker. You misled me into thinking she couldn't bake."

"I only said your sweets were better."

"I need to get back to my bakeshop."

"Give yourself a few more days. One of my servants put a notice up on the door so everyone would know you're sick."

"Thank you for taking care of everything and for helping me get better."

"It's been my pleasure."

The tiredness returned. She didn't understand why her body kept reacting this way.

"You're sleepy?"

"I'm sorry, it's been a lovely dinner but I am. I don't understand."

"Let me carry you back to your room."

"I can walk." She stood up but almost fell over. Mr. Steele caught her and picked her up. She laid her head against his chest as it was too much work to hold it up.

He laid her on the bed. "I will have the maids come in to help you out of your gown. Thank you for a lovely dinner." He held her hand and kissed it.

~

Noel woke to darkness. Had she slept through another day or was it the night of her dinner with Mr. Steele? She sat up and didn't experience any dizziness or fatigue, it must've been the food. There was water on the table by her bed, so she took a long drink then stood up. She opened the door and blackness greeted her. Noel wondered if she could find the kitchen and if her energy would sustain her through the walk. Her stomach grumbled with hunger.

Mr. Steele came around the corner. "Noel. It's two in the morning. What's wrong? Are you hungry?"

"Yes, I am."

"Go back to your room and I'll find you something."

She walked back and waited. Mr. Steele brought in a sandwich and fresh vegetables and sat in the chair next to the bed. She ate it all.

"I don't understand why I'm so tired." Noel sat the plate on the table.

"Your body must need the rest after everything that happened. It's all right, you're safe here."

Noel set her plate on the table. "I don't understand why I'm so sleepy. I've never been one to stay in bed for long, even when I've been sick."

Mr. Steele took her hand in his. "You've never been through something like this before. It's a nightmare, your husband left you for another woman and you were attacked. That's a lot to get through."

Tears filled Noel's eyes. Mr. Steele stood and then sat next to her on the bed. He put his arms around her and held her while she sobbed. He handed her a handkerchief, and she wiped her eyes and blew her nose. *How could Drake leave her?*

Mr. Steele touched her hair. "I'd love to make you my wife. I would always protect you and keep you first in my life, just like I've done these last few days." His fingers massaged her neck.

Noel fell under his spell again. She laid her head back against his chest and went to sleep.

~

A door shut and Noel opened her eyes. She heard voices talking, but she didn't understand what they were saying. Had it been last night she fell asleep on Mr. Steele or the evening before. The days had become a blur. She had to stay awake. Her stomach hurt from hunger. It must've been two nights ago. She had to go home.

She knew Mr. Steele was developing feelings for her, more than just an attraction. She couldn't return them and it'd be wrong to lead him to believe she might.

She put her legs over the side of the bed and stood. They trembled as if she'd run a long distance race. They held her weight. She quietly cracked the door open and peeked out.

Mr. Steele was talking to someone, who she guessed to be Doc Bradford. She wanted to hear what they were saying, but it was too risky, they might see her. She decided it best to get back in bed and pretend she was asleep in case they came to her room.

She barely made it in bed when footsteps stopped outside her door. She closed her eyes and slowed her breathing, but the hammering of her heart against her chest was uncontrollable.

The door opened. "Looks like she's still asleep. The sedative should be wearing off soon."

It was the doctor's voice. She hoped he didn't come any closer.

"When it does, we'll go up to my cabin. I hope to spend Christmas with her there." Mr. Steele's voice.

"Be careful on how much Laudanum you give her. You don't want to overdo it. I would start decreasing the doses once you get to the cabin."

"I will. I don't want to keep giving it to her. I have to get her away from here. Not many people know where my cabin is. She'll be safe there until I figure out the next step."

"I wouldn't wait too much longer. They've had men searching every day."

"Hopefully, with our dear sheriff out of commission, it will slow things down."

"I should return to my office, there's not much more I can do here. I've given you more of the drug."

"Thanks for your help Doc. I'll be talking to you soon."

Footsteps retreated, and the door closed. Noel peeked through the eyelashes of one eye. They had left, her room was empty. *I can't believe Mr. Steele is drugging me to keep me with him. Why? What did he do to Drake?*

Thoughts reeled through Noel's mind as all this

information had her rethinking everything. Steele must have hired the man to attack her. He'd carried her back to his house without any resistance from her. It made him look the hero by coming to her rescue so she'd rely on and trust in him to keep her safe. And to think Noel fell asleep in his arms the night before last.

How could she have been so naïve? She'd even entertained thoughts of misjudging him. Noel had believed Drake left with another woman and Steele cared for her.

Noel had to escape. Steele planned on taking her to his cabin, who knows where. She couldn't let him sedate her anymore, he must be mixing this drug into her water or food. A small window was high on the wall above her bed. Noel stood on her bed but barely reached the windowsill. She'd never pull herself up there in her weakened condition.

She had to find food and a way to escape. Her shoes were under the edge of the bed. She put them on and cracked open the door. No one was in the hall, so she tiptoed out of her room. She had no idea which hallway to take, so she walked the opposite direction from where Steele and Doc Bradford had talked. The house was dead quiet, she took each step slow and methodical. She dare not make a sound. After making it past a few rooms, it looked as if the kitchen was in front of her. Peeking around the opening, she didn't see anyone. She crept through it and out onto the back porch.

The porch was long and wide. The garden spread out from the bottom steps, if she made it to the other side, she'd disappear beyond the trees and bushes. Exhaustion set in, but she kept moving.

"There you are, my dear. I went to your room, but you were gone. Why are you outside? You should be in bed resting."

Noel jumped. Her skin crawled on the back of her neck. "I needed fresh air and I am ready to go home. Thank you so much for taking care of me." Noel took a few steps down before he grabbed her arm.

"It wouldn't be wise for you to go alone, what if the man who attacked you is waiting to finish what he started? I won't let anything happen to you. Let's go inside and have lunch, then if you still want to leave, I'll take you." He guided her toward the kitchen door.

Noel's mind spun as she searched for a way out. Steele rang a bell as they entered the dining room. A servant came, and Steele asked for lunch to be served. He pulled out a chair and Noel sat down. He poured her a glass of water. "They should be bringing us tea. I'm sure you're hungry after all the meals you've missed."

How could she not eat or drink anything? She had to play his game better than he did. A servant brought in sandwiches with carrots and apple slices. He poured two cups of tea from a pot and placed a bowl of sugar cubes and a small pitcher of cream by each of them. Noel reasoned the tea must be safe because the servant gave the same to Steele. She added sugar and cream and took a sip. It was hot but soothed her dry throat. She ate a few bites of her sandwich and pretended to drink the water.

Steele watching her intently as he ate his food

and drank his tea. "You aren't eating much."

"My stomach is upset. The sandwich is very good though." She leaned back and looked around. It was the same beautiful room they'd had dinner in the other night, too bad the man who owned it, was a monster in expensive clothing.

The servant brought out chocolate candies for dessert.

Steele picked out a few and popped them in his mouth then offered one to Noel. "This will make you better."

"I can't eat another bite, but thank you." Noel hated being nice to this man. He'd hired someone to hurt her and then drugged her. She had to act as if nothing had changed.

Steele put another candy in his mouth. "I do have a sweet tooth. That's what brought me into your store the first time. Since then, I've realized the owner is sweeter than her desserts."

Tiredness descended on her as it had many times before in the last few days. *Had he drugged her again?* She looked at what he had eaten and realized he never touched the cream. *Why hadn't she paid attention?* She would've slapped herself but her arms were too heavy. Noel knew the drug was already flowing through her body.

"Do you need to lie down? You look tired." Steele stood up.

"Maybe a short nap. Noel stood.

"I'll take you." Steele picked her up and carried her to the room. He laid her down on the bed. "Get some rest, your body is still recovering.

Noel laid back on the pillow trying to fight the

inevitable. Steele pushed her hair away from her face, his hand lingering on her cheek. He bent forward and kissed her. She wanted to throw up and slap him. *How dare he kiss me!*

"Sleep well, my dear. I'll check on you later. I love watching you."

The door shut. The man is crazy. *Someone, please find me!* Noel's eyes closed, and she faded from consciousness.

Chapter Nineteen

It had been three days since Drake had been off the sofa. Moving brought on dizziness, dizziness brought on nausea. Not much had stayed down. Violet took care of him during the day, and Albert at night. Drake slowly sat up to eat the pancakes and eggs Violet made for him this morning. So far, they were staying were they belonged.

Not being able to search for Noel was killing him. He'd had lots of time to think about who might've been involved with his wife's kidnapping and he kept coming back to one name, Steele. Drake knew he visited Madam Suzie's regularly, he beat up women and flirted with married women. Madam Suzie threatened Noel, but backtracked when he confronted her. She had to have threatened her knowing she had accomplices who would carry out her threats.

Could Steele have kidnapped Noel? The more Drake thought about it, the more it made sense.

Someone tapped on the door and Albert came

inside. "I've got news for you. Two days ago, I sent a wire requesting help to our governor. I received a reply this morning which said a Federal Marshal had already been sent to investigate the arson and murders committed here. I wired back that he never arrived. They immediately wired back a description. It matches the man we found in the river. I wired back we believe we found his body in the river, and whoever murdered him took his badge and identification. I received a telegram again, saying the state would be sending three Marshals this time."

"One mystery solved, a whole lot more ahead of us. I've been lying here wondering if all of these crimes might be related. And if so, who would have the influence and money to be the ringleader. The one name that rises to the top is, Steele. But what's his motive?" Drake slowly sat up.

"I need to get off this sofa and look for my wife. He could be directly responsible for her kidnapping, or at least knows who is. Madam Suzie threatened to harm my wife. We know she has a connection with Steele, probably because he financed her brothel. He abuses her girls, which is bad for business, yet she protects him. Drake stood up but immediately felt dizzy. "How can I function like this?"

"You need to rest Drake, doctors' orders. The mayor had me temporarily deputize two men this morning until the Federal Marshals arrive. We could demand to search Steele's home."

"We need more evidence, not just speculation. I don't think we should confront him, yet, I don't want him doing anything rash. However, we should assign one of the new deputies to watch his house and keep us informed of what he is doing." Drake massaged the back of his head with his hand. Even with pain medication, his head was pounding.

"I agree. I'll do that now. I think we might be on to something. Do you want anything before I go?"

"Can you have one of the men ride to the Crow camp? They can tell Kitchi what happened and why I haven't checked on Rose?"

"I will." Albert left.

~

Drake woke to Pastor Sheffield sitting with his eyes closed across from him. "Are you sleeping or praying?"

Pastor Sheffield opened his eyes and leaned forward. "You're awake. I've been praying for you and Noel. How are you feeling?"

"Better, but getting up makes my head spin. I need to find my wife." Drake stood. "The dizziness is a bit better. I haven't been up since it happened."

"I've been praying for wisdom and protection for both you and Noel. Sometimes, we're so distracted we can't hear what God's telling us. Maybe God's kept you on this sofa so you would listen."

"You've been a true friend, Pastor Sheffield. The only one I've confided in. You always encourage me with scriptures. If God loves us, why does he allow good people to suffer?" Drake's throat felt scratchy.

"God lets each of us make our own choices, unfortunately not all of us make the right ones. Men choose evil. Noel was taken by someone choosing to do evil. All we can do is pray for God's mercy to keep her safe and trust Him to help us find her." Pastor Sheffield sat his Bible on the table.

Drake coughed. "Would you mind getting me water, my throat is really dry?"

"You should've asked sooner. I'm sorry, I'm not a good nurse." Pastor Sheffield walked into the kitchen just as Violet came in the back door.

"Thanks, Pastor Sheffield for staying with him while I took care of a few things at home."

"I enjoyed it." Pastor Sheffield filled a cup with water from a pitcher on the table. They both walked into the sitting room.

"Here's your water, Drake. I should head home. I'm expecting to see you standing and walking when I stop by tomorrow. Violet, if you need anything please send someone for me." Pastor Sheffield waved as he left.

"Drake, I'm going to go cook dinner. Holler if you need something."

Pastor Sheffield left his Bible on the table. Drake picked it up and looked at the front page. He'd signed it and left it as a gift. As Drake opened it and flipped through the pages, he realized his head had stopped hurting. He'd be doing more than just standing and walking tomorrow. He'd be out on his horse looking for his wifel.

Chapter Twenty

Cold permeated Noel's consciousness, and she opened her eyes. She had no idea how long she'd slept, but Steele had moved her. She guessed it to be his cabin. She looked around and pulled the quilt closer. It had a stove, wash basin, table, two chairs, a sofa, and the bed she laid in. A small lantern burned but there wasn't a fire in the hearth.

She sat up as the front door opened, sending a colder blast of air into the frigid cabin. Steele walked in and dumped wood on the floor.

"You're awake. Let me get a fire started and then I'll explain why we're here. I'm sure you've been wondering." He stacked logs in the hearth and lit smaller pieces of wood with a match. Flames soon devoured the bigger logs.

Noel got out of bed and walked toward the fire. "Where are we?" She held her hands out to the flames and noticed her wedding ring was gone. *Had Steele taken it?* She couldn't have lost it.

"I brought you to my cabin to keep you safe. I

hate telling you this, but Sheriff West killed the prostitute he left with. They found her body out of town near a mine. They have a search party looking for him. I don't want him to hurt you too, Noel." He took hold of her hand and held it up. "I noticed your rings are gone. Doc Bradford may have removed them. I'm not sure where they are. Probably for the best so you won't have a reminder of him."

Her skin crawled at his touch. What a web of lies he spun. The saddest part about his scheme was, if she hadn't overheard the truth of what he was doing to her, she may have believed him.

He touched her cheek. "Do you remember our kiss the other night?"

Noel wanted to pull away but had to play along so he'd trust her until she found a way to escape. "I thought I dreamt it."

"Would it have been a pleasant dream if you had?"

"You've taken such good care of me." Noel had to find a way to try to change the tension. She thought of never seeing her parents again. Tears filled her eyes.

Steele wiped them away. "No tears. I plan on taking care of you for the rest of your life. Let me see what we can find for dinner. You must be hungry."

Did he plan on drugging her again, or would he let her stay awake since he had her in the middle of nowhere? "I'm not hungry."

"You should eat something, even if it's only a few bites." Steele started a fire in the stove and warmed up canned beans and sliced a loaf of bread.

"My cook sent food, so we should be fine for a few days."

Noel sat at the table. He put two bowls of beans down and scooted his seat next to her. She took a few bites to satisfy him and ate half a slice of bread. "Thank you."

"How are you feeling?"

"Much better."

Steele put the coffee pot on the stove to brew. When the pot finished percolating, he poured them both a cup. "You've been through a lot the last few days. I hope I've helped."

Noel smiled at him. She sipped her coffee without worry, knowing he was drinking out of the same pot. She even had another cup. He talked about where they'd travel. The heaviness of sleep returned. There must've been something in her bowl of beans. Obviously, he didn't trust her.

"I'm feeling sleepy, should I sleep on the sofa?"

"No, I'll sleep there."

Noel sensed his eyes on her as she made her way to the bed. She needed to get out of here, but not tonight. Darkness settled over her as she laid down.

~

The smell of bacon frying woke Noel. He must not have used as much of the drug as before. She had to relieve herself, and surprisingly, he let her go alone. The more he trusted her the better chance she had to plan for an escape. She went in and ate breakfast, she noticed he ate everything she did.

A man on horseback rode up to the cabin and

Steele walked outside to talk with him. After he left, Steele came in but didn't look happy. "I may have to leave for a few hours, but one of my men will stay with you. I hired them to keep an eye on the bank and my home, but someone broke into my house. I was right to bring you here."

"I'm thankful you've taken such good care of me." Noel lied.

Steele gently lifted her chin with his hand and looked her in the eyes. "Do you really mean that?"

"Yes, why wouldn't I? You've never left my side since that awful man assaulted me. You're the only one who has cared." She tried to keep the revulsion from showing in her eyes.

"I get the sense you still aren't sure about me." His thumb touched her bottom lip. "How can I show you how much you mean to me, Noel?"

"So much has happened, my feelings are confused. I'm thankful you've kept me safe." Noel smiled.

Steele leaned in to kiss her. Everything in her wanted to hit him. She moved her head to the side. He kissed her cheek.

"Can you give me time?" She looked into his eyes and tried to do her best acting. "I'm attracted to you but this is so fast."

"I'm willing to wait for you, Noel." Steele moved to the hearth and put more wood on the fire.

Noel heated a pot of snow to wash the dishes. She kept busy cleaning up the cabin until around noon when another man rode in. Steele again went out and talked with him.

"I'm leaving for a bit, Noel. This is Jake

Lundry. He'll watch over you until I return. I hope to be back by morning." Jake walked into the room. The stare from his heinous looking eyes bore through her sending chills down her spine. This man made Steele look like a preacher.

"Take me with you?" Noel pleaded.

"I can't. As I said before, it's too dangerous. You'll be safe with Jake." Steele grabbed his heavy coat and walked out the door.

In reality, Steele was the one she needed to fear. He never planned on letting her go. Jake sat at the table while Noel fidgeted on the sofa. Steele must have forgot to give her more drugs at breakfast. Every plan of escape she ran through her head fell short.

Jake left and came back with a bottle of whiskey. She guessed he planned on getting drunk. That scenario might be good or bad. He could pass out, giving her time to escape, or he could become aggressive toward her. She'd hope for the first choice.

Chapter Twenty-One

Drake searched every inch of Steele's house, but neither he nor Noel was there. The servants put up quite the fuss, but they didn't stop him. He had to find his wife.

He sat out of sight, observing the house from a distance. He expected there was someone watching him. Steele had to be a shrewd man because no one had found out all he'd been into until now.

Kitchi moved Flying Wind in next to Gunner. "Anything?"

"Nothing."

"You sure he have wife?"

"Almost positive. If he doesn't have her, he knows who does. I'd bet my life on it. He will come back here at some point." Drake took his feet out of the stirrups and stretched his cramped legs.

"Saw fire when almost to town." Kitchi pointed behind them.

"What!" Drake looked back and smoke billowed

up in the distance. "I have to make sure Noel isn't there but I also need to keep an eye on Steele's house."

"You go. I watch house."

"If he shows up, and leaves, follow him?"

"I not let him out of sight."

"Thank you, Kitchi." Drake turned Gunner and took off toward the jail. He alerted his deputies to gather townsmen and head to the fire, in case, they could put it out. Drake ran Gunner hard. He realized a pattern was forming, the fires were all within a few miles of each other.

Just like the other fires, by the time he got there, the fire had consumed everything. Animals wandered around. The smell made him nauseous, which wasn't hard after the last few days. His head started hurting again. Drake tied a bandana over his nose.

Drake's deputies and a small group of men galloped in. Deputy Albert shouted to Drake as he rode alongside. "Whose ranch is this?"

"It belongs to Mark Davis. Not sure if he was home." Drake dismounted to look for clues and a body.

A cloud of dust followed an unknown horseman as he rode toward Drake and his men. Seven guns pointed at him as he brought his horse to a stop. "Don't shoot, this is my ranch." He dismounted and walked over to Drake. "Who did this?"

"We don't know. Where were you?"

"I was hunting up on the mountain. When I came out of the trees, I noticed the smoke and rode straight here."

Drake picked up a half-burned torch from the dirt. "Where are your men?"

"I sent all but one home for Christmas. Shorty should've been here." Mr. Davis took off his hat and wiped the sweat from his forehead.

"There's a ranch hand missing Deputy Albert. Have your men search the property and what's left of the house and barn." Drake put his hand on Mr. Davis's shoulder. "Why don't you sit down a moment while we look? This is a huge shock to come home to."

One of the new deputies found a body and a couple of animal carcasses in the ashes of the barn. Mr. Davis broke down when he was told of the body. Drake had a hard time witnessing the man's grief. It made him think of Noel. What if she'd been murdered? He doubted he would survive that. Drake asked Albert to write down what they found. Noel hadn't been here for which he was thankful. He left to continue searching for his wife.

Gunner was breathing heavy by the time he got to town, so Drake rode home to retire him for the day. He rode back out to Steele's house on Wind Dancer.

When he got to the place where he left Kitchi watching the house, he was gone. Kitchi's tracks were almost hidden by the new snow, it had been increasing in intensity since the fire. He hoped Kitchi left markers as he followed Steele, at least, he hoped Kitchi was following Steele.

The sun had begun its descent in the west behind the mountain range. He might have to find shelter for the night while following Kitchi, he headed home to get supplies.

Chapter Twenty-Two

Jake drank himself into a stupor and passed out. Noel breathed a sigh of relief as snores filled the cabin. She had to act fast. Steele had been gone for a few hours.

She took Jake's coat from the hook and found an old pair of boots Steele must have left behind. The coat stunk like sweat but would help keep her warm. If she kept her shoes on and stuck them in the boots, they fit. She gathered blankets from the bed and folded them. Noel put matches, a few pieces of wood, bread, fruit and a small pan inside of them and tied it up. She wanted to take Jake's gun, but he had passed out with it in his holster, and she didn't want to wake him.

She snuck out the front door and ran to the stable where Jake's horse was. Noel took off on his horse at a brisk pace, not knowing where she was or which way to go. The snow fell fast, and it looked like it might turn into a blizzard. The sun hid behind the clouds and she had no idea which direction East and West were.

Noel rode for an hour or so and darkness began gathering around her. She looked for a rock overhang or fallen trees to get under. Her face was numb. All she saw was tree after tree, nothing to shelter her.

A couple of times she heard noises around her and fear tied her stomach in knots as her heart beat loudly in her chest. Did Steele and Jake follow her? No one appeared, and she kept riding.

If she had calculated her day's right, tonight would be Christmas Eve. She loved Christmas. *Noel wondered if she'd ever spend another one with Drake.* She pondered over the past year and especially the last few weeks. She loved Drake. Noel hated being alone. She had to laugh at that thought, as here she was, in the middle of the forest. Alone.

The forest became much more dangerous after dark. Her need for shelter increasing with each moment. Every part of her hurt from the icy temperatures. Her mind kept replaying the last week with Steele.

She lowered her head to keep the snow from pelting her in the face and continued pushing the horse onward. She caught herself subconsciously counting each step the horse made. When she reached one thousand, she looked up. It was almost dark. She had to find a shelter as she could barely move her fingers. She came to the edge of a hill and spotted some fallen trees in a clearing below. The hill looked steep, but she had to risk it.

Noel nudged the horse forward, but it resisted. She kicked it in the side and they went over the edge. Her horse sensed the unstable ground and tried to step back, but it was too late. Realizing he couldn't retreat, the horse panicked and ran. He violently crashed into some snow-covered rocks, one of his front legs sunk into a crevice, launching Noel over his head. She tumbled down the hill coming to a stop under a tree. She lifted her head but blackness sucked her into unconsciousness.

~

Noel woke not sure how long she'd been out. Her head and body throbbed from pain. She sat up and realized the horse had suffered a broken leg. *Are we both going to die here?* She saw the bundle made from blankets only a few feet from her. She crawled to it and untied the blankets. It took a while as her fingers were so cold. She wrapped the blankets around her and crawled back to the tree. Her eyes would shut for a few seconds and then pop open. *I have to stay awake.*

She looked around and saw a faint light in the distance. She was certain it hadn't been there a minute ago. Whether it be someone friendly or not, Noel had to make it there. If she stayed out here, she'd die.

She pulled herself up the tree trunk until she was standing and limped toward the light. She wished the horse didn't have to suffer. Noel fell multiple times but managed to get up and continue. Uncontrollable shaking consumed her body as she focused on getting there.

As she got closer, the light appeared to be inside of a building. Had she ridden in a complete circle and ended up back at the cabin? She focused her eyes through the falling snow and made out a steeple on the top of it. *Why would there be a church in the forest?* Maybe she'd come upon a small mining town. She had heard there were many in the mountains.

Noel made it up the steps to the large wooden doors. An intricately carved scene of a tree overhanging a river full of fish caught her eye. Beyond the river were mountains dwarfed by a doorway behind them. It was beautiful and must hold significance, but her mind felt muddled. Time was running out if she didn't get warm. She pounded on the door. No one answered. She turned the doorknob, and it opened.

A row of pews lined each side of the building with a walkway down the middle. Candles glowed in the sill of each stain glassed window. The windows were scenes from the Bible. Noel had read Bible stories even though she'd only been to church a few times in her life.

The stained-glass windows depicted Adam and Eve in the garden, Noah and the Ark, Moses and the Ten Commandments, David and Goliath, and four different pictures of Jesus, hugging the little children, walking on water, hanging on a cross and ascending into heaven.

Pine boughs around the candles filled the room with their woodsy aroma. Noel limped to where a wood stove heated the building. She sat in front of the fire, taking off layers as she warmed up.

Noel briefly imagined Steele or Jake finding her here, but for some reason that fear left. Peace settled on her the minute she'd walked into the chapel. Where was the pastor or caretaker? No one was here. She took the boots and her shoes off. Her feet and hands looked fine. No frostbite. She didn't understand how that could be possible, but she was thankful.

Her body longed for water as she could barely swallow. Noel didn't want to go back outside and get snow to melt. The warmth in the room seeped through the cold and she found herself getting tired. She laid in front of the stove and fell asleep.

~

The sound of piano music woke Noel. It was enchanting and calming. She sat up and saw an older man playing the piano. He was average looking with a white beard and hair and reminded her of her grandfather. He'd loved to play the piano too. The gentleman continued and paid little attention to her, almost as if he hadn't seen her.

Noel reflected on her childhood with her parents and how lonely she had been growing up. They were always too busy to spend time with her. Then she daydreamed of Drake. His responsibilities kept him away from her. It was the first time she related the two and realized she'd felt alone and forgotten most of her life. The people Noel loved the most weren't around much. She must've disappointed them.

The music stopped, and the older man walked toward her and knelt in front of her. He smiled, his gentle brown eyes spoke of his concern, putting her at ease. "How are you tonight, Noel?"

How does he know my name? Noel picked up one of the blankets she had laid down and wrapped it tightly around her.

"Who are you?" She asked.

"I'm the caretaker of this chapel."

Noel looked around. "Where's the minister?"

"There isn't one, this church is only for the lost to find shelter. Are you thirsty?" He stood up.

"I'm very thirsty. I didn't have the strength to melt snow." Noel watched him pick up a bucket by the piano. He scooped a ladle of water from it and handed it to her. She drank three ladles full before her thirst was quenched. "How many people find their way here, it's in the middle of nowhere?" Noel brushed hair back from her eyes and imagined how dirty and frightened she must appear.

"You'd be surprised, Noel, someone is always lost and searching for shelter."

"Did Steele send you?"

"No, he came here once, but ran away and found shelter in the dark places."

Noel shivered. *Had the fire gone out?* "How do you know my name?"

He gently took her hand. "I know everyone's name. You're very important to me." He placed something in her palm. "You've missed this."

She looked at the gold ring. The one Drake had put on her finger at their wedding. "How can you have my wedding ring?" Noel's eyes filled with tears. "Steele took it from me after he drugged me. I didn't think I'd ever see it again."

"After Charles Steele threw it in the lake, I

retrieved it for you. You've been through a lot. All the times you felt alone, you never were. I've been with you. I've seen all your tears and am aware of everything that's happened."

"What do people do when they leave here?"

"They either remain lost or begin a whole new life."

"I've never seen you before. How do you know so much about me?" Noel looked down, tears dropped from her eyes, and splashed one by one on the top of her feet. Something inside of her pulled her toward the words from this man. Her heart hammered as if it would burst in longing. "Am I dreaming or are you real?"

"I am very much alive and real. Everything I've told you is true. I sacrificed my life for you and each of those tears you're crying. Do you believe me?" He held out his hands and two round scars marred each wrist. "No one has ever loved you more than I do."

Sobs broke free from their restraints. "You can't be Jesus." Her heart beat against the wall she'd built around it. She took gulps of air in, trying to calm herself. This moment would define her life forever. His words spoke truth, and she wanted to learn more.

"I am Noel. Are you ready to be free? Truly free."

His words stirred inside of her, they created a longing and an understanding that this is how it was always meant to be. "Yes, I can't live being lost and alone anymore."

"You need only believe in who I say I am."

"I do Jesus, I'm so sorry."

He pulled her into his arms and she rested her head on his chest. Tears soaked his shirt as she cried out all the hurt and pain. Noel let go of a life full of disappointments and unforgiveness. She sobbed until she fell asleep. She was safe, and she was loved.

Chapter Twenty-Three

There were no visible horse tracks left for Drake to follow. All indications were Kitchi had headed into the mountains. He bundled up for the long cold night ahead of him. A lantern hung from the saddle horn to illuminate the darkness, but he'd have to take it slow.

There were pieces of cloth tied to trees every fifty feet or so. He could never repay Kitchi for his friendship. He'd saved Drake's life and helped him when he needed it most. The wind picked up and blew the snow sideways. It stung the exposed areas of his face. This was a brutal blizzard.

Drake was about to stop when he noticed a light ahead. As he got closer, it shone from inside a small cabin. He'd circled around back when Kitchi rode up beside him.

"Two men inside cabin. Much yelling. No one come out."

"Did you hear a woman's voice?"

"No, only men."

Drake dismounted his horse. "I'm going to get closer, so I can understand what they're saying. He snuck up to the cabin and crouched beneath the window."

He peeked in and noticed Steele talking with another man. Steele paced the floor and looked angry.

"Why did you fall asleep, you drunken fool? You let her escape. Even with your horse, she'll never survive in this blizzard." Steele pounded the table. "I don't need the likes of you." He grabbed his pistol from his holster and shot the man in the head.

Drake knew the man couldn't survive from that shot. He ran back to his horse. "Steele shot the other man in the head for letting Noel escape. I'd love to bust in and take Steele down now, but time is important. We have to find Noel before it's too late. She took the man's horse, but won't last long in this blizzard. Let's go!"

"Take horses and hide in bushes. I find way she go." Kitchi got off his horse and walked into the underbrush, but soon returned.

"Horse break branches in forest. She go this way."

They got on their horses, Kitchi lead the way. He found broken branches, trampled bushes, and horse droppings that gave him clues to the direction Noel traveled. Drake didn't know how she'd survive in this weather. He doubted she had taken much, if any, supplies with her.

There was no moon to light the sky, only

blackness, which had settled around them like a tomb. The white flakes swirled at a fast pace making it hard to see. They trudged their horses forward. Drake guessed it had been a couple of hours since they left the cabin.

"She go this way." Kitchi turned around and yelled at Drake while pointing.

Drake had a hatred burning in his gut for Steele. If anything happened to, Noel, he'd kill him. He kidnapped her, kept her in a cabin in the middle of nowhere, and now she wandered through the forest at night during a blizzard. He grasped for hope but knew the reality of the situation. Very few survived in this weather without the proper supplies.

"We stop. Too hard to know which way. Sleep till light." Kitchi dismounted.

Drake agreed. If they got too far off Noel's path, it would take much longer to find her.

They tied their horses to some trees, and Kitchi built a fire. "You sleep, I add wood."

"I can't sleep, but you should. One of us has to be alert to search for Noel tomorrow."

Kitchi had taught Drake a lot about tracking, but he was nowhere close to Kitchi's skills. Drake leaned back against a tree and tried to unwind. He pondered all the times he'd disappointed Noel, the missed dinners, and the days and nights away. He had to change things, he wanted to make it up to her.

Jesus, if you're listening, please keep my wife safe. I'm sorry I haven't been the husband she's needed. I want the chance to make it up to her. Forgive me. Show us where she is.

Silence greeted Drake's words. Did Jesus hear him? Drake had battled throughout his life on whether he believed Jesus loved him. His parents took him and his sisters to church a few times, but Jesus had never been a big part of their lives. Pastor Sheffield had opened his eyes to the possibility he'd been missing out on knowing Jesus.

Tonight he trusted if there wasn't a God, Noel wouldn't make it. If there was a God, she just might have a chance.

"She's with me."

Was he hearing things in the wind whispering through the trees? If Jesus spoke those words, did it mean Noel had gone to heaven? His heart sunk, and his stomach felt nauseous. He had to get control of his emotions.

Kitchi slept sitting up against a tree. Drake leaned forward and put more wood on the fire and wrapped the furs tighter. Their horses nickered, and Drake wondered what animals were hunting them. As long as he kept the fire going, they should be fine.

A star peeked through a cloud for a moment and he remembered it was Christmas Eve. The night chose to celebrate Jesus' birth. He never imagined he'd be spending it searching for his wife in a blizzard. He hoped the miracle of Christmas would shine on Noel tonight.

~

"Drake! Wake up!" Kitchi stood at the edge of the hill pointing down.

"Horse lying near bottom of hill."

Drake jumped up and ran to look.

"Horse look dead. Broken leg."

Drake and Kitchi made their way slowly down the hill to the horse. Kitchi was right. "If this was the horse Noel rode, she must not be far." Drake looked around, but it was a complete whiteout. Kitchi descended the rocky hillside to the bottom.

"Drake!" Kitchi pointed to a mound of snow underneath a tree.

Something might be under that mound. Drake ran to the tree, clearing the snow away to reveal quilts. As he pulled back the layers he saw Noel's face. He yelled to Kitchi. "It's her."

He fell to his knees and cradled her head in his hands. She moaned. "She's alive."

"I'm here." Kitchi knelt beside them.

Drake watched Noel open her eyes. "Where's Jesus?" she asked.

"What?"

"He was holding me in the chapel. Why am I outside?"

Drake looked around. "There's no chapel, Noel, only a small clearing.

"I noticed a light and walked toward it. I opened carved wooden doors. There were candles lit and stained-glass windows with pictures of Bible stories. I warmed myself by a stove and fell asleep. I woke to beautiful piano music being played by an older gentleman. But he wasn't an older gentleman. It was Jesus, Drake. When he spoke to me peace surrounded me. He held me in his arms and I cried. All the hurt and unforgiveness I'd been carrying within me went away. He loves me, Drake. I'm not alone."

"That's a beautiful dream, Noel." Drake helped her sit up.

"It wasn't a dream, it was real." She opened her hand to reveal her wedding ring. "Steele drugged me and took my wedding ring. Jesus gave it back to me last night." Noel's eyes were alive with a fire he'd never seen in them before. She believed she'd been with Jesus in a chapel, here, in the middle of nowhere.

"Do you have frostbite anywhere?"

"I'm fine. I've been warm since I entered the Chapel. Jesus gave me water too."

"You've been through a lot, Noel." Drake lifted her into his arms.

"Jesus said those same words to me. You don't believe me, do you, Drake?"

"You believe it, Noel, so it's possible. Let's get you back to town."

They walked back up the hill, Drake put Noel's arm over his shoulder and his arm around her waist so he could help her. When they got back to the horses, he boosted her into his saddle and then got up behind her.

Kitchi got on his horse and looked at Drake. "Great Spirit visit wife. Keep her safe."

"Thank you, Kitchi, at least one person believes me." Noel smiled at him.

"I didn't say I didn't, Noel. It's just, there's no chapel here now." Drake snapped the reigns and Wind Dancer started trotting.

"It was here, and Jesus was too." Noel leaned back against Drake, and it didn't take long until he heard snoring. She was worn out and needed to rest. His gut burned when he considered all Steele did to her. It was apt to get exciting when he got back to town. He wouldn't stop until Steele was behind bars or dead.

"Glad wife safe. Seems nicer." Kitchi laughed.

Drake smiled. "Yes, she does." *Thank you, Jesus, You are alive, no more doubts.*

Chapter Twenty-Four

Kitchi had left their house to return home to the Crow camp. They came back the long way so Steele wouldn't see them. Dr. Brown examined Noel and said it was a miracle she had no frostbite considering how long she'd been out in that blizzard. Drake intended to arrest and jail Steele today for his numerous crimes, including assault, kidnapping, and murder. He had to find him. He wanted to Noel to stay with the Sheffield's while he and the deputies went after Steele. Drake wondered what the Sheffield's would make of her time with Jesus.

They walked hand in hand toward the Sheffield's house behind the church. Halfway there, Drake slowed their pace, then stopped and looked into his wife's eyes.

"Noel, I've come to a decision I hope you'll like." He touched the wound on her neck and then kissed her on the forehead. "I'm resigning as sheriff after I ensure Steele is behind bars. I'll suggest the mayor promote Albert to my job.

I want to buy land near town, where I'll breed horses, while you run the bakeshop. With Wind Dancer, Gunner and Ruby we'll be off to a good start. Then I'll get another stallion and a couple more mares. There's some land not far from Mildred's that I've had my eye on.

"You'd be willing to give up being sheriff, a job you love, just for me?" Noel touched the side of his face.

"I should've done it long ago. I've had the mistaken idea the town couldn't survive without me. After being incapacitated for five days, and Albert taking over, I realized he was ready to handle the job. In times of emergencies, if he needs extra men, I'd volunteer if you were alright with it.

"Oh, Drake. Are you sure you'd be happy?"

"I know I will. I've fulfilled my dream of being a sheriff, so now let's discover what the next dream will be. I want to be close to my wife again and at home with her in the evenings. I've never stopped loving you, Noel, and I need to act like it. Maybe you will take a few days off so we can do things together. For instance, I think it's time we made a trip to Denver to visit our families."

A big smile came over Noel's face as she threw her arms around Drakes' neck and passionately kissed him. "I've never stopped loving you either, Drake. A trip home is long overdue."

"Let's not tell anyone about this yet. How about we invite the Sheffield's, Mildred and her family, Violet, and Albert over for a Christmas celebration tomorrow? I need to round up Steele today before he gets away."

~

Drake ran to the sheriff's office after dropping Noel off. It was urgent, he wanted to get Albert and the deputies together to take Steele into custody. When he arrived, the jail cells were full. "Albert, what happened?"

Albert got up from behind the desk. "We have the outlaws responsible for torching the ranches and murdering the McGregor's and Davis's ranch hand. This morning while we were out scouting, we caught them lighting a fire to the Smith's house and barn. We surrounded them and were able to hold them at gunpoint and tie them up. The Federal Marshals arrived today. They'll be taking the outlaws to Helena today. None of them are talking."

The door flung open.

"Sheriff! Come quick!" A man yelled and motioned for them to follow as he ran back out the door.

Drake and his three deputies, Albert, Rinderle, and Callahan, followed the man to Madam Suzie's brothel. They heard women crying as they entered the building. Doc Bradford hurriedly came down the stairs. "I was on my way to get you, Sheriff. Madam Suzie is dead."

"I bet you were Doc. Deputy Callahan, arrest Doc Bradford for kidnapping and drugging my wife."

"Hold on, Sheriff. I only gave her a sedative for her pain. There's nothing illegal in that."

"You were an accomplice to her kidnapping.

You were drugging her for the purpose of keeping her with Steele."

"Steele brought me to his house to help her with pain after she'd been attacked. He led me to believe she was there of her own free will."

"We'll let the judge decide. You're under arrest."

Deputy Callahan forced the doctor's hands behind his back and handcuffed them together.

"What about Madam Suzie, Doc? Did you kill her?"

"I would never kill anyone. My job is to help people not hurt them."

"Not where you're going. Get him out of here, Callahan." Drake motioned to his deputy.

Deputy Albert and Rinderle followed Drake upstairs to Madam Suzie's room. She lay crumpled on the floor surrounded by her girls. Some were crying, but most looked relieved.

Drake knelt beside Madam Suzie's body and checked for a pulse. Nothing. Red and purple marks encircled her neck. She'd obviously been strangled. Drake pulled a blanket off the bed and covered her. He stood and looked sternly at the girls "I know somebody here knows who did this. Someone came to visit her and one of you had to watch that person leave. Who found her?"

Della stepped forward. "She told me to come to her office after lunch and I found her lying on the floor. I screamed, and the other girls came running. Someone must have sent for Doc."

"I need all of you to tell the truth. If it happened to her, it might happen to each of you."

One of the women started sobbing. "Mr. Steele busted into her room about an hour ago. I overheard them arguing, so I listened at the door. Mr. Steele was very mad at her because she hadn't done what he wanted her to. He said something about her getting the men he hired out of town before they were caught, but she got greedy and had them burn another ranch.

Mr. Steel said he planned on foreclosing on those ranches and starting a cattle empire because they wouldn't be able to pay their loans after the fires took everything. He yelled, "He wished she wasn't his sister." Then it sounded like he hit her. I could hear her struggling and choking. When I heard someone fall, I ran, because if he caught me, he would kill me too."

"Steele is Madam Suzie's brother! He killed his own sister. I have more than enough evidence to hang the man. Deputy Albert and Rinderle, run back to the jail and get Callahan and meet me at Steele's house.

"Della, would you summon the undertaker to take care of Madam Suzie? I hope the rest of you will choose to make a better life for yourselves than that of a harlot. I'll be calling on most of you as witnesses to the crimes Steele committed in this establishment."

Anger pulsed through Drake's body. He wasn't waiting for his deputies. He ran to Steele's house. He had a score to settle, and it was personal. He snuck around to every window but didn't see anyone inside. The place looked deserted. He decided to check the barn.

The back door to the barn had been left open. He quietly walked in, moving from stall to stall. He froze as he heard someone talking. He moved closer, crouching down.

Drake peered through a crack in the stall. It was Steele. He was mumbling to himself as he saddled his horse. Drake pulled his gun and stood up, pointing it at Steele's head. "Come out here with your hands up. Don't try anything, cause I'd love nothing more than to put a bullet between your eyes."

"Sheriff. How nice of you to come to my going away party. Too bad I won't be staying for it." Ha! Steele yelled as he smacked the horse in the rear causing it to kick the stall door open and knock Drake backward to the ground.

Steele dove on Drake, grabbing his gun arm and banging it on the ground until he knocked it from his grip. They grappled in the dirt, each of them trying to reach for the gun. Drake smashed his elbow into Steele's face, sending blood spattering. Steele broke free, and they both jumped to their feet. Steele lunged, swinging wildly, missing his mark, then rushed head first into Drake, burying his shoulder into his chest, slamming Drake into a wall. Steele's face sneered in anger, "I'm going to kill you." Steele put his fist into Drake's ribs causing an audible groan to emanate from his gut. Drake countered with a fast straight punch, landing his knuckles into Steele's cheekbone snapping his head back, and knocking him off balance. Sweat mixed with blood dripped from Steele's face. He faked a left punch and sent a roundhouse at Drake's jaw, sending him backward to his knees. Instantly, he felt a gun barrel pushed into his forehead.

"Not bad, Sheriff, but looks like I win. First your wife and now you. I enjoyed her company, it's sad she ran away and met her demise. We would've made a charming couple, her and me. Such a beautiful woman, you really should have treated her better. But, it's too late." Steele cocked the gun.

"She's alive." Drake waited to die.

A shot rang out, but Drake didn't feel pain. Steele fell like a tree, hitting the ground with a loud thud, a bullet in the back of his head.

Deputy Albert appeared from the shadows. "I got you a Christmas present. I hope you like it."

Drake stood up, his knees shaky. "I couldn't have asked for a better one. I owe you."

Albert slapped him on the back. "Bozeman just got a lot better with the likes of him gone."

Drake checked Steele for a pulse. None.

"I'm going to get Noel at Pastor Sheffield's. It's Christmas, and she and I need to spend the rest of it together. I've got something important to tell you, so I want you to come over tomorrow and we can talk about it."

Chapter Twenty-Five

Noel and Drake sat in front of the fireplace sipping hot tea. Snowflakes fell outside their window. So much better to be inside and warm then in the freezing snow. There were times during the last week she wondered if she'd ever see Drake again or even if she wanted to. Lies might have changed her life forever.

Last night Noel escaped from an evil man intent on destroying anyone who got in his way, only to be lost in a forest freezing to death. Then she saw the light in the chapel. When Noel told the Sheffield's what happened, Mrs. Sheffield teared up and declared she'd been part of a beautiful and unforgettable miracle.

Drake now knew the entire story of what took place, from the man who assaulted her outside the bakeshop, to when Kitchi and he found her in the forest. Drake stayed silent the whole time, but she saw the emotion in his eyes when he said a voice told him, "She's with me." How he'd promised Jesus there would never be another doubt if He was real if she made it back to him alive.

Noel snuggled into Drakes embrace. His ribs were sore, and his face bruised from his fight with Steele. She thought about what he went through today and her eyes welled with tears. He'd be dead if it wasn't for Albert. She pushed in closer as what she could've lost overwhelmed her. Another Christmas miracle.

The sound of his heart beating helped calm her still frazzled spirit. Flickering flames consumed the logs in the hearth, sending dancing shadows and heat into the room. Warmth and safety… she'd never take them for granted again. In the chapel, Noel had sensed perfect peace and unconditional love, a feeling she would never forget.

"Are you falling asleep? Drake hugged her close. We should go to bed."

"Never sleep on the sofa again. I need you next to me every night." Noel stood up and Drake grabbed her hand. Coco stretched on the chair while Maggie and Tucker barely lifted their heads as they walked upstairs.

Drake lit a fire in the bedroom hearth. She remembered the last time they'd been in this room together with Drake lighting a fire. Her cheeks got warm. She put her arms around her husband's neck. Drake looked into her eyes.

"Aren't you tired, Noel? The last few days have been unimaginable."

"I want nothing but you Drake. I want it to be the way God intended for us. We can sleep in tomorrow."

Drake didn't need another invitation. They kissed each other with renewed affection. She wanted him to know how much she loved him. She understood he loved her and how scared he'd been at the thought of losing her. His kisses trailed down her neck. He desired her and never wanted to be away from her. He wrapped his arms around her waist and pulled her closer. She thanked Jesus for giving him back to her. Tonight would be their new beginning.

~

Sunlight pierced through the white lace curtains covering their window. Noel woke up. Her head rested on Drake's chest. His breathing was slow and even. She tried to move without waking him but he opened his eyes and pulled her back to him. He smiled, and her heart melted. This man made goosebumps cover her skin with just a look.

"I need to start cooking for tonight." She whispered.

"It can wait a bit longer."

~

Noel pulled the ham out of the stove to baste it. Drake sat in the kitchen telling her about Rose. She'd been the one who first alerted him to Steele violently abusing the women at Madam Suzie's. He'd wanted to tell Noel about Steele, but it never seemed to be the right time when they'd had a few minutes together. Rose was the only one of Madam Suzie's girls willing to testify against Steele. She'd feared for her life, not only from Steele but from Madam Suzie and the henchmen. Drake had to hide her somewhere while he gathered more evidence. He realized if he acted sooner, things might be different now, but possibly not for the better. Noel understood he hadn't been meeting other women, he was trying to protect them.

Tomorrow they'd go to the Crow camp to tell Kitchi what one of the deputies overheard. The men hired by Steele had talked of the Crow woman they'd beaten and how she'd deserved it. One more charge to bring against them so they'd all experience the end of a noose.

They would be bringing Rose back to be with the girls remaining at Madam Suzie's. The women would have to build new lives. They should change the place into a hotel and café. Bozeman needed another place for families to stay and eat. They would have to redecorate it but for the ladies who had nowhere else to go, it meant being able to survive.

Drake also wanted her to see how the Crow lived and learn more about their culture because Kitchi was his brother in every sense of the word. Drake talked about the missionaries who dwelt close to the Crow and taught them the skills they'd need to survive in dealing with the white man. They also shared Jesus with them.

She wanted Kitchi and his family to be welcome at their home. Kitchi would be a great advisor to Drake on the best horses to buy. Most people in town would probably not accept him, but she didn't care. Kitchi proved his loyalty and friendship to her husband and now to her.

~

Everyone arrived for their Christmas celebration. The aroma of ham, fresh bread, and various types of pie filled the air. Laughter was present in every chair in their house.

Noel wore her favorite brown taffeta gown with the heart pendant from Drake around her neck. Drake was handsome in his black pants and vest with a crisp white dress shirt underneath. He glanced over at her and winked, so much had changed between them in just a few days. She'd even caught herself dreaming of having a little boy that looked like his father.

They'd taken their places around the table when Pastor Sheffield asked for everyone's attention, then prayed over their meal.

After the prayer, Drake stood. "Can I also have everyone's attention, please? I just wanted to let you all know, and especially my good friend, Deputy Albert, I've decided to quit as sheriff of Bozeman. This is the best decision for Noel and me." Everyone in the room stopped talking. "I spoke to the mayor and recommended Deputy Albert be promoted to sheriff.

I've come to realize as much as I loved being the sheriff, I love my wife a lot more. The job kept me away from her more than it should have, and with all that's happened to Noel and me lately, it was time to make a change. I've always wanted to own a horse ranch, so I'm going to go after that dream, which means I'll be home with this beautiful woman every evening." Everyone smiled and talked amongst themselves about how happy they were for

Drake and Noel, and also for Albert.

Drake continued. "While Noel and I have discussed this decision, there is another surprise I have for everyone, this time for Noel as well."

Drake took Noel's hand and scooted his chair away from the table. He knelt on one knee looking lovingly into her eyes. "Noel West, I'd let my job and all its responsibilities come between us. It took a miracle for me to realize how much you mean to me. I can't imagine life without you, and I love you with all that I am. I look forward to enjoying every day of the rest of our lives together. Will you honor me by marrying me again tonight?"

Noel wiped tears from her eyes and threw her arms around Drake. "I'd love to."

Most of their friends wiped a few tears away as well and then congratulated Noel and Drake.

"Pastor Sheffield will be performing the ceremony after we eat."

They enjoyed their dinner and waited for the wedding.

"Can we all move to the sitting room?" Drake held Noel's hand as they followed everyone. Pastor Sheffield's wife Alma had snuck out and lit dozens of candles around the room in preparation for the ceremony.

The room smelled of pine from the heat of the candles around the evergreen boughs Drake had brought in since they didn't have a chance to put up a tree. Pastor Sheffield led them in their vows of love and commitment to each other.

"You may kiss your bride."

Everyone clapped and cheered as they kissed.

Drake kissed her neck below her ear. "I'm thankful God's grace brought us to a place of forgiveness. I love you with all my heart, sweet Noel."

Epilogue

Cries woke Noel from her slumber. She picked up their baby from the cradle next to the bed. Drake rolled over, and she laid her up against him. Two-month-old Grace Nicole stuck her thumb in her mouth and was sucking away. Noel had learned from experience she wouldn't be pacified for long.

Noel guessed she'd conceived last Christmas when they'd found their way back to each other. Jesus blessed them with the most perfect gift on that day. She never tired of watching her husband look into their daughter's eyes. Grace held onto her father's pinky with her free hand and Noel knew he wouldn't deny her anything.

They'd moved into their new home right before Thanksgiving and now were sharing Christmas with all their loved ones. Both of their parents came up to spend time with them and baby Grace. Their home had five bedrooms and Noel hoped one-day children's laughter filled them all.

Everyone who'd shared Christmas with them last year would return along with Kitchi and his family. Kitchi's sister, Hurit, married a few months ago, so their family grew too. They might need to add more space to their dining room.

She pulled back the curtain from the window. Snow fell in soft big flakes. Their barn was not quite finished, so all their horses were in the pasture. Two new foals were born last spring. One from Gunner and Ruby, and the other from Wind Dancer and Kitchi's stallion, Flying Wind. Drake recently traded some work for three mares and a stallion, they were expecting more foals this spring.

"Noel, come back to bed, your daughter needs you."

Whimpers came from the little bundle as Noel sat down to nurse her.

"I am a blessed man to have two beautiful girls in my life." Drake sat up next to Noel and rubbed her back. "What did you get me for Christmas?"

"I won't tell." Noel turned her face toward him and smiled. "You'll have to wait."

"It doesn't matter, I have all I need right here." He kissed her forehead and laid back down. "Wake me when you're done. I can't wait to open my gifts." He laughed.

The End

Keep reading for the first chapter of A Healing Heart

Chapter One

1894

The train car door swung open as gunshots rang out. Sophie's eye's popped open as her mother screamed. Her father jumped to cover her mother with his body. He told Sophie to stay down.

A man rushed into the car his eyes wide with fear. He wore the red uniform of the train attendants. "Everyone stay seated and remain quiet! Outlaws boarded the train at the last station and have the conductor at gunpoint in the engine compartment. They're demanding the contents of the safe."

Another woman screamed and others broke down.

"Please everyone, remain calm! Don't attract attention to us. Hopefully, they'll take the money and leave. If they hear a commotion back here, they may check what's going on." Cries subsided as the attendant walked down the aisle past each bench.

Sophie's eyes locked on the car door, unaware that fear kept her from exhaling. They didn't have a way to defend themselves. The pressure building inside her caused her forced its way past her lips and she gasped for more air.

A gray-haired woman spoke up. "Sir, there are orphaned children in the rail car behind ours, did anyone warn them?"

"Yes, Ma'am. Another attendant went to tell them."

Without warning, the train lurched forward as the brakes screeched, tossing everyone about like a ball between two boys playing catch. Sophie caught herself before she fell into her mother's lap. Her heart pounded against her ribcage so loud she could feel it in her ears. Panic froze the faces of the surrounding passengers into strange expressions.

A distant pounding noise grew in volume outside her window and she peeked out. A gang of masked outlaws on horses neared the train. It didn't look good. More gunshots rang out. Children from the car behind them cried. Sophie refused to speculate about what might take place if a gunman broke into their train car. Her father didn't carry a gun. She doubted if any of the men in this car did. Sophie had wanted to learn how to handle a gun before they headed west but never followed through on it. If she had, she wouldn't feel so vulnerable.

Her father would attract attention. He dressed every bit the influential man he was, from the tailored suit to the expensive pocket watch attached to the gold chain and his shined leather shoes. His law practice in Philadelphia was the most powerful law firm in the city. Her mother wore the latest fashions and conservative was not part of her fashion sense. Sophie wished they could change into less conspicuous clothing.

Her uncle in Texas warned them that train

robberies were becoming more frequent, but Sophie never imagined it could happen to them. She assumed if robberies were increasing the presence of lawmen on trains would increase too.

Men shouting erupted outside the train. Sophie peaked out the window but couldn't understand what was being said. Two gunmen carried an injured man toward the outlaws on horses. One gunman looked toward her window and she ducked down. Curiosity could be a bad thing.

A gunman with a bandana over his face burst through the door of their car. "I need a doctor! Is anyone a doctor?"

Everyone glanced at each other, expecting someone to speak up. The silence was deafening.

The outlaw swung his gun from one side of the car to the other. "Since no one is responding, if I find out you've lied, I'll shoot you and your family."

Sophie struggled to stand but her legs gave out. Fear clenched her stomach and she could hardly breathe.

"Sit down, Sophie." Her father whispered. "You don't know what they might do to you." Charlotte, Sophie's mother, clutched her daughter's hand.

The outlaw walked toward her. "Sit down. I'm looking for a doctor, not a girl."

"I am a doctor." Sophie's voice trembled. *What am I doing? Please help me, God.*

"You're claiming to be a doctor, Now, that's funny lady." The outlaw paused, then pointed his gun at Sophie's father. "Are you trying to protect him? I don't have time for games."

"Do you think I'd draw attention to us if it wasn't true? I'm not playing games. I graduated from the University of Pennsylvania with a medical degree and I'm on my way to help my uncle with his office in Texas." Sophie's voice grew stronger with each word.

"That's quite the story miss." The outlaw grabbed Sophie by the arm. "All right, since no one else is speakin' up I guess you're the lucky one. You better be good, cause the boss don't like disappointment." The man pulled her down the aisle toward the door. Sophie's mother yelled. "Bring her back here!"

The man hurried Sophie down the steps. Her father brought her medical bag and handed it to her. "Don't hurt my daughter." He starred at the outlaw grasping her arm.

The gunman pulled Sophie toward the man on the ground. Blood seeped through his shirt and puddled in the dirt. It didn't look good.

An outlaw got off his horse and walked toward them. "Why did you bring this woman out here?"

"She claims to be a doctor, on her way to Texas. No one else spoke up. She's all we have."

Sophie went to remove the handkerchief over the injured man's face.

"Don't touch that, if you want to get back on the train." The outlaw above her shouted.

"I need to listen to his breathing." Sophie pulled her shaking hand back. She assumed he must be the gang leader.

"You'll have to do it through the bandana."

Sophie's hands trembled as she unbuttoned the

man's shirt. She could barely push the buttons back through the holes. Sophie took a few deep breaths to calm herself. She had to gain control of her emotions and concentrate on what needed to be done. Blood pooled around her fingers, she knew this man's life was flowing out before her.

Sophie pulled his shirt apart and discovered that the bullet wound was on the upper right side of his chest. She breathed a sigh of relief as she put pressure on the hole to stop the bleeding. "Would someone roll him on his side so I can see if the bullet passed through?"

The two outlaws next to her rolled him onto his side. The back of his shirt was covered with blood and dirt, she saw the exit wound. "It looks like the bullet passed straight through and missed his lungs, which, thank God, is good news." Sophie took pre-cut bandages out of her bag and placed them over the back hole.

"I don't believe in God." The gang leader snarled.

"It might help you if you did." The words escaped Sophie's mouth before she thought about the wisdom in saying it. She dared a quick glance up. The outlaw didn't smile. "Does anyone have whiskey?"

"I do." One gunman pulled a flask from under his vest.

Sophie poured it on clean bandages, then on both sides of the wound. The injured man moaned but didn't regain consciousness. She cleaned both wounds with the whiskey-soaked bandages before stitching his chest and back closed. Sophie finished by bandaging the wounds with clean dressings.

She handed the gunman more cloth bandages. "Remove the soiled dressings every day and clean the wound with whiskey-soaked bandages before applying new dressings. I think he'll pull through, but he shouldn't be traveling for a few days." Sophie gave a bottle to the man. "If he runs a fever, you'll need to put a small amount of this in tea or water and have him drink it twice a day."

"Why wouldn't I take you with us to look after him?" The leader knelt next to her. "It could be fun having a pretty doctor around to treat our aches and pains." He laughed.

"You said I could go back to my family if I didn't take off his bandana. I could've stayed silent and not helped. You would've never guessed I'm a doctor. I've done all I could to save him." Sophie looked into the dark brown eyes of the stranger. A shiver ran down her back as her confidence slipped. This man couldn't care less if he kept his word.

"You sound pretty sure of yourself. I've killed men just because I wanted to, but lucky for you I've never made a practice of killing women unless they got in my way." He stood up. "You better get back on that train before I change my mind."

Sophie gathered her supplies and closed the bag. She touched the injured man's forehead one last time. It felt cool. "Make sure you give him lots of water."

"Let's get out of here. We're done." The leader motioned for two gunmen to lift the injured man in front of one of the outlaws already on his horse. They galloped away.

Sophie crumpled to the ground as the last of the outlaws faded in the distance.

Her father startled her as he knelt beside her in the dirt. "You are brave. I wish you hadn't put your life at risk. I've never prayed so hard before. If the robber died, it would have served him right. There's a little boy on the train who is injured. He had a bullet graze his arm."

"The robber will pull through if they take care of him. He lost a lot of blood, but the bullet went straight through. I had to give my fear to God or I would've passed out. Father, I've never experienced such evil as when I looked in their leader's eyes. I didn't think he'd let me go." Sophie grabbed her father's hand, and they stood.

"Let's check on the little boy. It was torture watching it all and knowing I couldn't do anything. I understand now why you wanted me to carry a gun, sweetheart. I need to purchase one and ask your uncle to show me how to use it. You should learn too. It's dangerous out west.

Just say the word and we'll go back to Philadelphia. You can live at home until some man sweeps you off your feet. The hospital would love to have you there or I could help you buy an office where you could see patients."

"Father, I can't do that. There are too many doctors in Philadelphia. I need to stay with the plan I've prepared for. Philadelphia is not without danger. We lived where it wasn't as common but it existed. Although, I never feared for my life there. Will the train be able to run?"

"I heard someone say we'll be moving on soon.

Thank God they didn't kill the conductor. I don't know how many injuries there are other than the boy. You may be busy."

"What would I do without you, father?"

"Unfortunately, you'll find out when your mother and I head back to Philadelphia. Although, it won't be for a while. No need to dwell on it now."

This morning she hoped to become a doctor. This afternoon she became a doctor but would Nacogdoches be ready for a woman doctor?

She hoped Texas would be more acceptable of a woman doctor. It would be a difficult road ahead, but she felt ready for the challenge. Today she'd been forced into the fire, pulled herself together and relied on her training. There wasn't any reason to expect she couldn't continue doing the same.

She hoped the injured outlaw survived and thought about why he'd been given a second chance. She had prayed for him softly while she stitched his wounds closed and hoped he'd heard.

Darlia Sawyer grew up living in many of the western states during her childhood. She now lives in Western Colorado and considers it to be a blessing. Beautiful scenery, rich history and great weather to enjoy it all in.

She lost her husband of twenty years in 2004 after dealing with medical issues his whole life. Her relationship with Jesus and her daughter and two sons helped her through those days.

She married Ken in 2007 and together they have three boys and three girls, just like the Brady Bunch. All the children are now adults and they've added two son-in-law's and two adorable granddaughters to the family. Next year we'll be adding two more grandbabies and a daughter-in-law.

There have always been two constants in her life. The love and strength found in her relationship with her Heavenly Father and her love for writing and history.

The support from her husband, Ken, has given her the opportunity to follow her lifelong dream of writing full time.

She hopes her writing will inspire hope, a passion for life and the chance to once again believe in miracles.

To find this book and others by Darlia Sawyer, visit her at:

https://amazon.com/author/darliasawyer

Also you can follow her on Amazon and other social media"

https://www.facebook.com/DarliaSawyerAuthor
https://twitter.com/DarliaSawyer
https://www.instagram.com/darliasawyer

www.ingramcontent.com/pod-product-compliance
Lightning Source LLC
LaVergne TN
LVHW012019060526
838201LV00061B/4378